D1575329

ALEX
VAN HELSING

VAMPIRE RISING

ALEX VAN HELSING

VAMPIRE RISING

JASON HENDERSON

An Imprint of HarperCollinsPublishers

HarperTeen is an imprint of HarperCollins Publishers.

Alex Van Helsing: Vampire Rising
Copyright © 2010 by Jason Henderson
www.harperteen.com

Library of Congress Cataloging-in-Publication Data
Henderson, Jason, 1971-
    Vampire rising / by Jason Henderson. — 1st ed.
        p. cm. — (Alex Van Helsing ; bk. 1)
    Summary: At a boarding school in Switzerland, fourteen-year-old Alex Van Helsing
learns that vampires are real, that he has a natural ability to sense them, and that an
agency called the Polidorium has been helping his family fight them since 1821.
    ISBN 978-0-06-195099-5
    [1. Horror stories. 2. Vampires—Fiction. 3. Supernatural—Fiction. 4. Boarding
schools—Fiction. 5. Schools—Fiction. 6. Switzerland—Fiction.] I. Title.
PZ7.H37955Vam 2010   2009039663
[Fic]—dc22   CIP
                                                                                  AC

Typography by Joel Tippie
11 12 13 14   LP/RRDH   10 9 8 7 6 5 4
❖
First Edition

For my mother, Trudie Lee Bell Henderson

CHAPTER 1

Alex Van Helsing ran. He ran instantly and without a second thought in the direction of the scream, bursting from the side of the road into the trees as fast as his legs could move, rubber soles churning against soft earth and leaves slick with dew. The sun had barely risen, and in the woods it was still dark. He heard the shout again—someone screaming out hoarsely, a voice that sounded raspy and male.

Alex had been walking the tree-lined road that ran from the gate of his new school, shivering slightly in the predawn cold. He'd been at Glenarvon Academy for all of two miserable days, and already he could tell he was going to have to make a change. Unable to sleep, he'd snuck from his bedroom and out, through the deserted hallways and then the grounds and the front gate, onto the road. Not far away, he could hear the distant sound of loons on Lake Geneva, the occasional croak of frogs. Other than that, all had been silent but his own soft, steady breath.

Then the scream from the woods split the air.

Alex picked up his pace as the sound grew more desperate and then cut out. Running, he wove his way under low-hanging branches, one of them smacking his ear.

He leapt over a log, reached a clearing, and froze, stumbling to a halt.

There in the woods, he saw a body.

It was male, probably in his forties, wearing a boat painter's cap and overalls. The victim's beard was drenched in blood, and there was steam rising off the body. Even without the scream Alex had followed, he knew—this death had just occurred.

Alex's eyes darted around the clearing and back to the body. He was not afraid of the dead; at fourteen he had already trained in mountain rescue in Wyoming, had already participated in search operations. Some of those had ended badly. But nothing he had seen in Wyoming had ended like this.

Then came another sound: *static*, a jagged, dark whisper in his brain that jolted his head for a moment. Alex blinked, staggered by the feeling, losing his balance for a second. *Set it aside. Pay attention.*

A wisp of leaves curled and lifted, and Alex's eyes flicked toward the movement. Then he saw something that raised the hairs on the back of his neck: A figure in white slid behind a nearby tree.

In that split second he saw that it was a she, and she started to run.

"Hey!" Alex shouted, taking off after her. She was insanely fast. "Hey!" he called again, leaping over underbrush, gauging the ground and the trees and the branches with every running step.

She might have been involved, might be a witness, might be a scared daughter or girlfriend. She must have seen something. Now and then Alex could glimpse, by trickling early light, a leg here, a flowing sleeve there, now nearly a hundred yards away. *Catch her. Catch her.*

They broke into another clearing and she was exposed in the dimness. This time she had nowhere to go—she had reached a rock formation that cut off her escape and now she spun around, slapping her hands back behind her against the rock, facing him.

As Alex slid to a stop he took her in: white boots, white tunic, white leggings, even a short, white hood.

She wore white gloves—no, not gloves, those were her hands, bone white as well.

"Hey," Alex said a third time, less forcefully. His brain was buzzing more strongly now, whispering and pounding against the inside of his head and against his eyes and contact lenses, and he swallowed the feeling down.

She was leaning forward, mouth barely open, teeth clenched. Her eyes were so dilated that they shone. She stared wildly at him, and he thought for a moment that she had been severely traumatized and struck dumb.

He said gingerly, "Do you know what—"

And now she snarled, and as she opened her mouth, he saw that her teeth were enormous, white and sharp. Not quite teeth. They were fangs.

Alex felt his own mouth hang open, and he was already twisting, finding his footing as he spun around, and running as she leapt at his back.

It wasn't a girl, it was an it, he thought, still unwilling to believe. *It wasn't a girl; it was a thing. That's crazy. That's crazy and it's at your back!* He felt her close behind as he ran through the trees. Rapidly he tried to retrace his steps. He didn't know these woods. He had just followed a scream because it was the right thing to do and he had no idea—

Feet churning, *Don't look back, she's still there, I turned this way—the road is that way.*

He could hear the road, a few hundred yards off. He could hear early morning traffic. Alex turned toward the sound, losing his footing for a second. He reached out to steady himself but overbalanced.

Slow motion. Falling, he began scanning. As he smashed into the forest floor, his face just missed a long, narrow tree limb lying on the ground. Alex grabbed the limb, lifting it as he rolled, bringing it around as the girl leapt for him.

He swung the limb around, catching her in the knee, and her momentum sent her sprawling past him.

As she hit the ground she tumbled and righted herself. He was still trying to rise when he saw her taut muscles bunch through the white leggings and she jumped at him—her sharp nails catching him in the shoulders.

Alex felt the air shoot from his lungs as she drove him back against the earth. His mind raced. *The world won't slow down, but your mind can. What do you do?*

She tried to pin him—close now, her face an arm's length from his, his shoulders and shoes digging into the forest floor. But he wouldn't be pinned. Not now. Alex swept his feet out and around her legs, then to the side, and she lost her balance and fell. He rolled, kicking her away, and now she did a wondrous thing, he had to admit: While still in the air she spun like a cat, *like a freaking cat*, and she was coming again.

Sharply, Alex realized that she wasn't just the random attacker or tweaker at the beach he'd prepared for in self-defense classes. She was something else. And there was something else in him clicking in on how to deal with her.

He felt himself reaching for the downed limb again, certainty driving his actions as surely as certainty had driven him off the road to pursue the scream.

In the fraction of a second as she leapt, Alex brought the limb in front of him and locked his arms. He felt it drive into her chest as she landed.

Her face registered shock and anger. She was snarling, white eyes blazing in the dimness, and then she was on *fire*.

A moment later, she burst into dust.

Alex kicked and crab-walked back as the cloud of dust settled over him, landing on his slacks and shirt. He got to his feet, shaking his head: *No, no, no. This doesn't happen.*

He ran for the road, staggering out of the woods and tripping, spinning onto the asphalt.

A flatbed delivery truck swerved around him, barely missing him. As Alex rose, still staring into the woods, he realized the driver was yelling at him in French.

The driver stopped shouting when he took in the sight of Alex—torn and muddy pants, scrapes and cuts from the trees. Alex gestured mutely, *Can I have a ride?* even as he was grabbing the edge of the truck bed and jumping on.

"Where do you need to go?" the driver asked in French.

"My school—*école*," Alex answered in his beginner's French. "Um, Glenarvon. Glenarvon Academy."

He watched the woods race by the half mile back to the gate, all the while thinking, *This doesn't happen. This didn't happen.*

CHAPTER 2

An hour and a half later. Alex was in the headmaster's office, wearing fresh pants and a clean shirt. His mind was still swimming with the nightmare—no, the *thing* that happened—and that wasn't even what had brought him here. He'd have to come to terms with what had transpired in the woods, and he didn't have the time yet.

"I want a new room," Alex said flatly.

There. He had said it, after working up the courage to walk the long corridors, hearing the clapping of his dress shoes against the marble floors. With every step he had gone over it in his head. He knew what he had to say. And then at the last second he changed it.

"I . . . I mean, I need, I—I think I need a new room."

Alex squirmed as the woman behind the desk—draped in a shawl as if they didn't keep the foyer of the headmaster's office toasty and warm already—eyed him through her glasses. Mrs. Hostache, he reminded himself as he read the nameplate on her neatly arranged desk. Next to the nameplate was a bud vase, and in it a white flower he didn't recognize.

Mrs. Hostache cleared her throat. Off to the right behind her stood the door to the headmaster's office. Over her left shoulder Alex saw a massive window revealing a view that could have been a painting: the leafy grounds of Glenarvon Academy, and beyond, the waters of Lake Geneva, cold and gray with early autumn. He got lost in the view for a second, waiting for her to respond. He had started this badly. *Lemme go out and come in again,* he thought.

"What was your name?" Mrs. Hostache peered through wide, blue-rimmed glasses that threatened to hide her face.

"Alex. Alex Van Helsing."

Mrs. Hostache leaned forward, chin on her fist, seeming almost amused. Her hair was brown, pulled back in a tight bun, wisps of gray streaking through it. She chewed her lip. "Didn't you just get here?"

Alex nodded. "Yeah, I—I got here two days ago." So she did remember, he thought with relief. It was already two weeks into the fall term when he had come in, all of a sudden sent here by Dad and Mom because after the incident at Frayling Prep they hadn't known what to do. Now he was in a new school, new house. New room.

"What seems to be the problem, Alex?"

"I . . ." Alex thought for a second.

He had found a dead mouse in his bed. He wasn't afraid of mice, but you had to admit that was pretty nasty. He was further unnerved because he hadn't woken up with it, not that sleeping with a dead mouse would have been better. No, he had awoken around four A.M. and realized that his alarm clock had been unplugged. His roommates, the Merrill brothers, or Merrill & Merrill as they were called by the other students, were pretending to sleep.

Sick of being there with them, Alex had risen and washed his face. He dressed and nearly gave up trying to put in his contacts, the cursed things—he had to try three times to get the right one to go in—and quietly exited the school, out into the darkness to walk. He was done with them.

And then the nightmare in the woods. He could still feel the ferocity of the girl in white's attack. He had returned in a mild state of shock, only to find the mouse, tiny, fragile, and dead, on his pillow.

Coming off the trauma of the attack, he had wanted to throw up. He wanted to throw up now, thinking about the mouse, its tiny closed eyes, a tiny body someone had snuffed the life from just to make a point. He was more horrified by Merrill & Merrill than by the nightmare in the woods; he had just faced something that *did not happen*, in the words his father always used, and now he had returned to find that there were also monsters in his room: his roommates. After two days of penny-ante antics like busted alarm clocks, toothpaste in his shoes, and glue in his books, they now seemed to be turning sadistic.

"I found . . ." *Wait. Careful, Alex.* He thought down the chessboard a few moves as he stared into the giant, slightly amused eyes of Mrs. Hostache. If he told the story he might trigger some sort of investigation, or whatever it was they would do here. He pictured the Merrill brothers, Steven and Bill, with their kind eyes and cruel mouths, fessing up or not, and it wouldn't matter, because within three days of his arrival Alex would have caused a major disciplinary event. He might even get swept up in it; the brothers might be able to turn it to their advantage. Everyone would hear, and watch.

"I found that I snore," he said quickly. "And it disturbs Merrill and Merrill—I mean, the Merrill brothers. I think they would be happier if I . . ."

"What's this?" came the voice of Headmaster Otranto, now standing in the open door of his office. Otranto was a wide-shouldered, older man, Italian with a finely trimmed mustache, wearing a topcoat. He was headed out.

"Oh, you have a message." Mrs. Hostache rose, handing Otranto a slip of paper. She turned away from Alex, and he listened as she and Otranto lowered their heads. "In the woods . . . asking us to keep a watchful eye." Alex took this in. Did they know about what had happened to him in the woods this morning? Was he walking into more than he had thought?

But no. Otranto frowned and nodded, then changed the subject. "Is there a problem with this one?" Otranto looked Alex up and down, as though he were leafing quickly through the files in his head.

"Young Master Van Helsing is thinking he would like a new set of roommates."

Alex felt himself flush. Otranto had seen his file, had heard the whole story of what had happened at the old school. On Alex's first day, Otranto had given him a long lecture. "What happened before is of no concern to me, young man," he had said. "But it bears a mark, a mark of character, shall we say. And that mark must be proven to be a smudge, and not a scar." Which was a weirdly charming way of saying it was of *great* concern.

"What happened?" Otranto asked.

"Nothing, I just . . . we have differences."

"And are you certain, sir, that you do not invite these differences?"

Alex stared, his eye twitching. What do you say to that?

His right contact was killing him; he now suspected he might have put it in inside out, which meant it would bother him until he had the chance to take it out and try again.

"I didn't invite—" he said. "I just think that we made the assignment pretty fast, and I thought maybe I could be matched, somehow."

"Matched? *We* made the assignment?" Otranto repeated the phrase, the temerity of it.

Alex looked down.

"I think we should . . ."

"I think you should be getting to class," said Headmaster Otranto. "And *we* will look forward to more of your learned consultation in the future."

Alex sighed heavily.

Out of the foyer and into the corridor he slunk. First period had already begun. The year was off to a fine start.

Feeling like a mouse himself, Alex entered his first-period classroom. First period was literature, and Mr. Sangster, a teacher in his early thirties with close-cropped, slightly curly hair, was at the board, scrawling on the chalkboard. Alex scanned the room and found his desk, not far from the back. Glenarvon was a school for boys, so it was a rather smarmy, sarcastic, hostile horde that looked back at him. They were a privileged assortment. Sons of diplomats, aristocrats, and oil barons mingled with the children of high-level corporate executives from around the globe.

And then there was Alex, who was far from under-privileged, but whose old-money background was boring and staid and on the very low side of rich. Unlike the others, he wasn't here to make lifelong connections. He was here because he had been kicked out of his old school for something that still haunted him, and sent here by his father, who had covered up the whole incident and told Alex to forget it ever happened. But how could he? Alex was still grappling with the guilt.

He walked slowly past two boys he had met—Paul, a friendly, beefy British boy who seemed to have crammed himself with great discomfort into his chair, and Sid, who was Paul's roommate, a gangly Canadian with red, unkempt hair. Alex had already hit it off with these two at lunch on his first day, though the conversation had run little past their amusement over Alex's "exotic"—it really wasn't, he insisted—last name.

Alex stopped at his desk and felt the eyes of Bill Merrill on him, in the seat right next to his. Bill's brother, Steven, was on the other side of Bill. Alex glanced over; Bill was smirking, a smirk that Alex had seen could charm teachers into missing the cruelty that hid there. Alex laid his backpack on the desk.

Sid looked back as Alex pulled out his chair. "Where have you been?" he whispered.

Alex shrugged. "Otranto's." He started to sit down.

There was no longer any chair, he realized. In a split instant he was falling, his arms flailing—and out of nowhere Alex felt a strong hand grab his collar and catch him.

He looked up, bewildered. There, with one arm holding Alex's entire weight aloft, was Mr. Sangster.

How fast had the teacher moved? Had he already slid around to the side of the class as Sid had been whispering to Alex?

"You should be more careful." Mr. Sangster had crinkles

around his eyes, which looked almost merry and angry at the same time. Alex found his footing as Mr. Sangster let go.

The whole class was watching as Alex grabbed his chair and sat, staring at his desk. Why was this happening to him? What had he done? But then he remembered, and the flush of shame came again, and again was stifled.

With the stifling came a rush of hot anger as Alex looked at Merrill & Merrill. Bill had pulled out his chair. Alex was sure of it.

Mr. Sangster was moving again, toward the front. Like Alex, and unlike most of the students, who tended to be from Europe, Asia, and the Middle East, Mr. Sangster was an American. "I think, before the acrobatics of young Master Van Helsing, we were discussing *Frankenstein*."

Alex pulled a notebook and a thumbed copy of *Frankenstein* from his pack. Mr. Sangster had told them he was a Romantic and Victorian connoisseur, and that he intended the study of *Frankenstein* to take several weeks.

"So," said Mr. Sangster, "what sort of stories did the Villa Diodati group tell?"

"Vampire stories," Alex heard Sid mutter.

Alex looked at Sid. "Say it," he whispered. Sid shook his head. Apparently Sid was into vampires. He had been *thrilled* to hear Alex's name was Van Helsing, even though the name meant nothing, really.

Bill overheard Sid and spoke up: "Vampire stories."

"Eh," Mr. Sangster said. "Not really. But close. What were they writing?"

Bill threw Sid a punishing look. "You moron, you gave me the wrong answer," he said under his breath.

Sid reacted as if he'd been hit. He whispered, "Honestly—*two* of them *were* writing vampire stories."

Mr. Sangster looked in the back. "Do you guys have something you want to add? Sid?"

Sid was dumbfounded for a second in the spotlight and trailed his fingers over his desk. After a moment he managed to drag forth, "Polidori and Byron were writing vampire stories." Sid had named two of the people at the house party the teacher was going on about.

Mr. Sangster shrugged. "Well, that's not what Mary Shelley says."

They were talking about the introduction to the book. Not even the book. The introduction, where Mary Shelley talked about getting the *idea* for the book. Alex scanned the length of Shelley's *Frankenstein* and calculated that at this rate they would still be reading it when he left for college.

"Ghost stories," offered Bill. "Scary stories."

"Right," said Mr. Sangster. He pointed out the window, out to the trees on the grounds. "In 1816, just across this very lake, in a charming villa rented by the famous poet Lord Byron, a small party decided to pass the time telling ghost stories—or so reports Mary Shelley."

Sangster looked up at the board, where he had written a number of key words and names. "The party at the Villa Diodati that summer—the Haunted Summer—consisted of five writers: Lord Byron and Percy Bysshe Shelley, who were already quite famous; two young women writers, Mary Godwin (soon to be Shelley) and her half sister Claire—whom Mary disliked so much that she doesn't even mention Claire was there; and Byron's doctor friend, Polidori, who wrote short stories. And they're bored out of their skulls, because although it's summer, a massive volcanic eruption in Asia has clouded the sky and made the weather everywhere cold and rainy. So Lord Byron issues each of them a challenge: Write the scariest, most terrifying story you can.

"Mary says the famous guys each wrote some minor pieces, and that Dr. Polidori had, and this is fun, 'some terrible idea about a skull-headed lady, who was so punished for peeping through a keyhole—to see what I forget—something very shocking and wrong of course.'"

Mr. Sangster looked back at the names. "And then they—gave up."

"Maybe it was the skull-lady story," said Bill. "Polidori sounds like a loser."

The class laughed. Bill was a crowd-pleaser.

"Yes," Mr. Sangster said softly. "He does sound that way." Then Mr. Sangster turned back to the class. "But out of Byron's challenge, a seed grew—and that seed would germinate in the wild imagination of nineteen-year-old Mary into one of the most *resilient* books in the history of the language. This one. *Frankenstein*." He smiled.

Alex dared to raise a hand. "Not one of the *best*?"

"We'll see. But it happened here. Right over there at the Villa Diodati. You all enjoy quite an honor, reading it next to its germination."

The bell rang. "Tomorrow we begin," said Mr. Sangster, and the class started to file out.

Alex wanted to turn back to apologize for being late but Mr. Sangster had already turned to a notebook and was scrawling in it. At the door Sid was asking, "What was that about with Bill?"

Alex looked at Paul and Sid as he adjusted his backpack on one shoulder. He didn't know the pair that well but he felt himself desperately clawing for friends. "You won't *believe* what happened," Alex said.

A hand clamped down on his shoulder and Alex thought for a second that Mr. Sangster was yanking him up again, but it was Bill. "You should be more careful," the smiling boy said, his brother sneering next to him. "So, Van *Helsing*. Kill any *monsters* lately?" Bill hissed the syllables out with disgust.

So Alex's name was Van Helsing. *Yes, we all get it.* Like *that* Van Helsing, the vampire hunter from *Dracula*. But Alex's father was a professor and his mother was an artist. The only great meaning to his name in all his years was carried in the ornate lettering on annual reports from the Van Helsing Foundation his father controlled. It was a name of some renown in philanthropic circles and turned up occasionally as a sponsor of public radio programs he never listened to. There was no brandishing of wooden stakes, no demons or vampires.

Not a one, not ever. "That is not how things are," his father had told him once. "Those were things that just didn't happen," and they never touched on it again. But of course now Alex was sure that his father had been wrong. Or else that he himself was going insane.

Which might be the case. He had felt entirely, blissfully normal until recently, back at Frayling Prep in the

United States. Short bursts of fuzzy pain behind his eyes, a feeling he could only describe as *static*, had started intermittently and then grown, jagged and buzzing. Alex had gotten a little paranoid. Then the incident that had gotten him expelled. Now he was here. None of this was stuff he would say to Bill Merrill.

Alex turned to Bill. He couldn't let the mouse incident go whether he was getting a new room or not. Alex spoke softly because the door was still ajar, Sangster just beyond. "I know what you did."

"Oh?" said Bill. His brother listened silently. Alex had slept in the same room with them for two nights and he hadn't heard Steven Merrill say ten words. The two of them clearly didn't want him in their room, but they couldn't come out and say it; they had to make his life miserable. "And what did *you* do, eh?"

Alex noticed that Sid and Paul were watching intently, and so were some other boys passing by. Bill came closer: "What did you do that got you kicked out of your last school? You set something on fire? Steal something? I'll bet that's it."

Paul moved his own massive form into the space. "Come on," the British boy said to Alex. "Let's go."

Alex surveyed the scene, his eyes twitching again. Bill had his backpack hanging casually over his shoulder, an expensive model with countless cords and loops hanging down. Alex shook his head. "We don't have to do this," he said.

"We don't have to do this *here*," said Bill. "How about later?"

"Secheron," whispered Steven.

"Yeah," said Bill. "Good one, Steve."

"Wow," Alex referred to Steven. "He speaks."

"Secheron," Bill repeated, by which he meant a small village nearby. Alex had heard there were cafés, curio shops, and ice cream there. It all sounded charming. "After school."

Steven raised an eyebrow. For the first time Alex got the impression that still waters ran deep. "Football."

"Oh, right." Bill consulted his brother, casual and businesslike. "Practice. You think . . ."

As they were discussing when to beat Alex mercilessly, and whether their weekday soccer schedule could accommodate the beating, they now really did resemble Merrill & Merrill, a law firm. There was nodding and finally Bill turned back. "Friday. Day after tomorrow. Secheron."

Paul said, "Oh, you're going to *fight* in Secheron? Where, at the ice-cream parlor?" Paul turned back to Alex. "Come on," he repeated.

"Fine," Alex said, feeling exhausted. "Secheron." He

rubbed his right eye, feeling some release when he pressed on it. As his vision cleared he rested his eyes on the cords dangling from Bill's pack.

The boys all started to leave.

Suddenly, Bill Merrill was mysteriously yanked back and smacked his head on the doorjamb. He yelped sharply. "Hey!"

As they continued briskly down the hall, Alex smiled. Sid said, "What the—?"

Alex shrugged. In the moment before they moved, he had taken just a few seconds to loop one of the cords of Bill's pack to the hinge of the door.

"I am more than just a mouse," muttered Alex.

CHAPTER 3

From the moment Alex had walked in the first evening, he had understood the situation by the way Merrill & Merrill arranged themselves, Bill standing like an unhappy guard, Steven leaning against a bookshelf and staring at the floor. They wanted a three-man room to themselves. For the first blissful weeks of the term, the brothers had been lucky; whatever curious fate had failed to fill their room, they had grown used to the luxury, stacking the third bed with DVDs and magazines and books. And then Alex had arrived to disrupt their paradise.

By now he had already learned to stay out of the room as long as possible. Let the Merrills have it. Let them study or not study, watch movies on Bill's portable player or not, but for the love of all that was holy, don't go back there until it's time for everyone to go to sleep.

Tonight he hit the library. The school was quiet in the evening, and the largest group he saw as he passed through the halls was gathered in the student lounge, watching local news on a large TV. Alex lingered at the entrance for a second, catching some of what apparently Mrs. Hostache had been whispering to the headmaster. A boat painter had been murdered in the woods, the third seemingly random attack in the past month.

That was the dead painter he had seen himself. He felt a pang of remorse over not reporting it, and yet for the life of him he had no idea how he would describe what he had seen—and what he had done. *How can I explain that I impaled someone with a tree branch—but don't bother looking for her?* He blinked it away. Now the incident was drifting into the past, into what he had to admit was denial that had taken him through the day without thinking about the girl with the eyes and the fangs, and oh yes, the cloud of dust. Come on. Maybe that had been an illusion—some sort of hoax. It simply, absolutely could not be what he feared it was. *Like Dad said, "Those things don't happen."*

The painter's murder itself was far from unique. Alex

had heard that people disappeared around here, not constantly, but a steady trickle. He had felt sure this was probably true but no more true than around any large lake. Now he was lost in too much knowing with no explanation.

Great place to send me, Dad. Sure can pick 'em.

The going wisdom on TV seemed to be that everyone should be extra careful at night. That advice sounded wise.

Alex found a table off to the side of the dark-paneled, shelf-lined library and hauled out his books. He cracked into *Frankenstein* first, reading the introduction and then moving into the novel, trying to drop into Mary Shelley's prose.

His eyes were bleary. After a moment he stopped reading and reached into his pack, pulling out his contact lens case, a bottle of cleaner, and his glasses. Delicately he began the process he had only recently learned, prying each eye open with his fingers and pinching the contact off his eyeball. "That's just weird," his younger sister had said when she first saw him doing this over the summer when he got them. "Nothing about touching your own eye is normal."

This was true. Putting the contacts in was agony, taking them out defied all instinct to *not touch your own eye.* He had to grab at the left one, the one that felt comfortable, three or four times before his thumb and forefinger found traction, and finally he felt the contact slip off his eye, now red with irritation.

Alex closed the contacts into their tiny case and donned his glasses, feeling much younger. Wasn't that what the contacts were really about, after all? He was just a boy with glasses, and then his mom had offered to get him these things. He looked older with them, strangely, and for the first time in memory he had peripheral vision. But was seeing a door before you bonked into it worth the punishing ritual of poking your own eye?

"I didn't know you wore contacts." Sid plopped down in the seat across from him. He had with him an enormous black-and-red paperback book, *An Encyclopedia of Vampires*, and a small stack of magazines and source books that Alex saw ran the gamut from horror to the supernatural to mythology, and segued as if in some geekish solidarity into science fiction and fantasy. He had no apparent school-related material at all.

"Well, I've only been here three days," said Alex.

"Does it hurt, touching your eye like that?"

"Yes," Alex said ruefully.

"Why do you do it?"

"I have no idea."

"What are you lot talking about?" said Paul, joining them. He had his copy of *Frankenstein* with him as well but dropped it as he sat, and started thumbing through Sid's magazines. "You got any *Cinescape*?"

"Do they even make *Cinescape* anymore?" Sid smirked. He was flopping open his massive encyclopedia and Alex saw that he had several sheets of graph paper inside. Each graph page had been divided into four sections, presenting a complete history on a person, and Alex looked closer: a picture, a name, and various descriptors like age, height, weight, and paragraphs on history, powers, and abilities. Sid selected a couple and said, "I was asking Alex why he wears contact lenses, if he hates poking himself in the eye."

"For the girls, mate, for the girls," Paul said. He looked around. "Oh, wait . . ."

"I don't wear them to get girls."

"Well, then you shall not be disappointed." Paul looked at Sid's graph paper and picked up a sheet, waving it at Alex. "Do you believe this? Look at this paper."

"What is it?"

"It's a character." Sid took the graph paper back.

"He spends hours—bloody hours, every day—designing characters. And not just characters, but *vampire* characters. For the Red World."

"The Scarlet World," Sid corrected, irritated. "It's an RPG." Alex vaguely knew what he meant: a role-playing game, the old paper-and-dice kind.

"*Scarlet* World," Paul acknowledged. "Now, no one else here plays this game, so he doesn't actually play the characters, he just makes more of them up. Each one has a race—"

"Class," Sid said.

"Sorry, a *class*. Smart vampires, dumb vampires, zombie vampires. This one is a rat vampire, I think." He held up a character.

"That would be a Nosferatu," said Sid, "you know, like in the silent movie *Nosferatu*. And he does attract vermin, so Paul has apparently learned more than he lets on."

"What's that one?" Alex pointed at the one Sid was drawing, a tall vampire with Asian eyes.

"It's a *dhampyr*," Sid said, excited. "A half vampire, you know, with a human mom and vampire dad. Like in *Vampire Hunter D*."

"What's that?" Alex asked.

"It's an anime. It's awesome."

Alex was amazed at the breadth of Sid's hobby. "You really got into today's class," he said.

Paul beamed at his roommate with something like

pride. "He could *teach* the class."

Sid seemed to fold this over before him and then he sighed. "Mr. Sangster's wrong, by the way," he said finally.

"About what?" Alex said curiously.

"Byron and Polidori did write about vampires," Sid said. "Mary just lies. That whole thing about Polidori writing a story nobody liked, about a skull-headed lady looking through a keyhole? That's stupid. You can look that up and you won't find it. Mary just put that into her introduction—sixteen years after the Haunted Summer—to make Polidori look like an idiot."

"See?" Paul said. "Listen to that. Like they're friends of his."

Sid was looking down, laughing, small and wiry and sheepish. For a moment Alex wondered if Sid minded being teased.

Paul concluded, "How I ever wound up hanging with such a nerd is a mystery."

"You're the one who's reading his space magazines," Alex said, smiling.

"True." Paul leaned back, the back of the wooden chair creaking with his weight. He kept the magazine open but looked at Alex. "So how on earth did you wind up rooming with Merrill and Merrill?"

Alex shook his head. "Luck of the draw."

Sid was working on one of his characters, a young punk vampire with stylish black clothes and haunted, puppy-dog eyes. "What are you going to do about Secheron . . . are you going to go?" Sid didn't look up from his drawing as he spoke. The very idea of the fight seemed to make him nervous.

"Am I going to *go*? That makes it sound like a sock hop." Alex felt an overwhelming rush of sadness and dull defeat, as though he were caught in a river that ran from his old school all the way here. "I can't *not* go," he said finally. "I can't. That would be . . ."

"Wussy," Paul said.

"So I gotta. I'm going to show up and see what happens."

"Can you fight?" Paul leaned forward.

"Not really," Alex lied. "Can you?"

"You've got to be kidding," said the giant boy. "I'm the size of a house, nobody ever tries."

Alex exhaled. "How hard can it be?"

"That's a good point," said Paul as he turned to Sid. "After all, why should the Merrills know how to fight either?"

Alex had to admit this might be true; the Merrills' bullying might be an elaborate front for cowardice. But somehow, given the penchant for violence they'd shown so far, he doubted that.

"They're mean," said Sid, as if reading Alex's mind. "They'll be able to hurt you whether they know any insane techniques or not."

Alex thumbed his book's pages like a flipbook and slapped the cover closed. "Gee, fellas, this has been swell."

Paul laughed. "'Swell' and 'sock hop' in two minutes. Is that how all Americans talk, like an old movie?"

Sid looked up. "Maybe he's an alien who learned to be a kid by watching old movies."

"If I were an alien, maybe I'd know how to fight," said Alex.

"If you were an alien," countered Paul, "you wouldn't tell us if you did know how to fight—otherwise you wouldn't go to Secheron."

Alex sat back. "You guys wanta come?"

Sid and Paul consulted each other silently. Finally Paul said, "Friday at Secheron, a fight and some ice cream? We wouldn't miss it for the world."

When Alex returned to the room for curfew it was ten o'clock and both Merrills were in bed awake, watching him from the bunk bed they shared—Steven above and

Bill below. In the darkened room, lit only by streams of moonlight through the window, they watched Alex in silence as he removed the stacks of DVDs and books that they had placed on his bed once more. Their eyes followed him as he went in the bathroom and shut the door, and returned and crawled into bed. After a while, Alex felt the tension slip away. He lay awake until he was sure they were sleeping soundly, and then drifted into sleep himself.

At half past one Alex awoke with a start. He could still see the lingering vestiges of a dream of his own father, shaking his head sadly as he came out of the meeting that formally ended Alex's career at his old school. Alex lay awake, staring at the ceiling.

It had been warm and sunny outside in the dream. He had been crying, honestly crying, wanting to feel his father's hand on his shoulder. And then he was freezing—and it was the freezing that brought him awake.

The Merrills were accustomed to Switzerland in the fall and had probably set the AC on blast just to spite him, for now he lay awake and saw his own breath in the moonlit room. He had one blanket, and as he looked over he saw that the Merrills had bundled up just for the occasion. This was just petty. He wondered what they might have done with the extra blankets in the closet, and the various options made him shudder.

And then he felt it—that static, that jagged shock to the back of his eyes, a tinny and unintelligible voice calling out.

That feeling, more than the slight scratching sound at the window, caused him to dart his eyes across the room.

There in the window, forty feet off the ground, someone was watching him.

CHAPTER 4

Alex rolled out of his bed, his arms and legs coiled and tense as he stared with blurry, nearly useless vision at the window. The shape that hung there was whitish, ghostly, and seemed to be swaying with its own weight, its arms splayed out like a spider. But more than this, it was upside down.

Alex grabbed his glasses, which he kept just under his bed next to his shoes. As he brought them to his face he saw the shape more clearly—a hood hanging down, arms holding tight to the edges of the window.

He could see her eyes. It was the girl from the woods. No, that wasn't possible. Another one, this one with yellow hair. She was watching him.

Alex glanced at Merrill & Merrill, who were still sleeping. He bolted for the door.

Barefoot, Alex ran rapidly down the hall, following instinct to find his way to a staircase that led up six or seven steps to a door outside. He knew that the moment he opened the door he would be breaking all kinds of rules.

So be it.

Alex threw the door open into the night, his own breath visible as cold air struck him. He stepped out onto a kind of battlements, a long walkway with a high stone side that circled the roof of the building.

Across the grounds, the moon shimmered on the surface of the lake. Alex had gotten lucky about one thing in his housing assignment—his house, Aubrey House, had a great view.

He hurried back along the battlements as fast as he could, the stones leeching warmth from his bare feet. He reached the edge of the battlements and leaned over, peering toward the sheer wall where his own window stood.

She was still there. She hung like a lizard, upside down, scuttling slowly from window to window. He watched as her bone white fingers found purchase between stones and on the edges of metal windowsills. She was staring through each window, cocking her head, which caused her hood to sway back and forth. If she had breathed, she would be leaving patches of fog on the glass. There was something crablike about the way she clung to the wall and moved jerkily along the stones. The static in Alex's mind was vibrating feverishly.

Just then, Alex scuffed his foot against a stone on the roof and gasped before he could stop himself. Suddenly the upside-down creature moved like nothing he had ever seen.

She flipped over, scuttling along the wall, her head whipping around, and he watched her white eyes sweep directly toward him.

She opened her mouth—*fangs* again, like the one in the woods—and hissed angrily. Then before he had a chance to blink, she leapt for him.

Alex reared back as she hit the top of the battlements, her leg muscles coiling under tight leggings. Her claw-like hands grabbed him by the throat and her white hood fell back, revealing spiky yellow hair and a youthful face. Her mouth was open wide, fangs bared in front of a grayish, bloodless tongue. She lifted him off the stones and smacked him against the battlements.

Do something. That was what he had learned in his self-defense classes. *Move. Never freeze. Answer the* questions. *What's going on? She's choking me. What do you have? I have nothing.*

What do you have?

I have myself.

Alex brought the palm of his hand up and smacked hard against her neck, right under her jaw. She lost her grip for a second and he twisted against the battlements, bringing his hands together and whipping them against her side.

She growled in anger and spun him around, and Alex put his hands on her shoulder blades, pushing. She was impossibly strong. His fingers latched on to her white tunic and dug in, and then she brought up her legs and kicked him.

The force hit Alex in the chest like a train, and he felt himself flying through the air.

Alex's hands went up to his glasses as he landed on the long, clay tiles of the roof, high above the battlements.

The roof was steep but not impossible. Alex found a foothold exactly as he would have done on a rock face in Wyoming, and waited. Below, she was a bobcat now, and she wanted him for dinner.

Alex scanned the roof. He got up and started running for the highest point, where he saw a weather vane clattering in the wind and lit by moonlight against the clouds.

The creature—all right, the *vampire*, one of those things that *do not happen*, according to his father—hit the roof and started bounding toward him. Alex looked down, running his fingers along the roof tiles. They were heavy and solid, about two feet long and made of red clay. He reached for the edge of one tile and yanked it, feeling the tar adhesive stick. It wouldn't come loose. She was coming fast.

Alex yanked again and the tile came free as she leapt. He slashed out with it, smacking her across the side of the head. The tile was heavy and rough on the edges, and pain shot through his hands as it ground into his fingers.

Still holding the tile, Alex ran for the weather vane as the vampire rolled down the side of the roof, howling in anger. He hit the vane, hanging on to the wooden housing where the iron device was bolted into the roof. There was nowhere else to go.

Down the roof the creature righted herself and began bounding again. Alex dropped the tile and began yanking on the weather vane back and forth, grabbing one arm of the vane right next to the *N*.

He pulled with all his weight, bracing himself with his feet. The vane tore free, wood and bolts flying, but as it came loose he lost his balance and began to fall.

He was sliding down the tiles. He looked to the side

and saw her coming fast.

All right. He had done this before at Jackson Hole, sliding backward on his shoulders, out of control. *What do you do?*

Alex yanked his shoulders forward and to the side and spun, painfully digging his heels and the weather vane into the tiles until he scraped to a stop. His bare feet sang with pain.

Then she was on him. The vampire growled and Alex whipped the weather vane over, smashing hard against her shoulder and neck.

This time she was hurt—the creature yelped and fell back.

Alex watched her crouch there for a moment, black blood streaming where he'd slashed her.

She spat, "You do this a lot?"

Then she snarled, coiled her legs, and leapt away. After a bound or two down the roof, she disappeared into the night, headed for darkness.

Alex was breathing hard, near hyperventilating.

What. Is going. On.

After a few minutes he started to move again, gingerly making his way down the roof until he found a low spot where he could drop down to the battlements. It was only when he felt the cold of the stones that he remembered he was still barefoot. His feet were filthy and covered in minor cuts, but all told he was fine.

For now.

He paused for a moment, listening. Could it be possible that the ruckus hadn't been heard through the thickness of the roof? But even after a few moments, no one appeared, no alarms sounded. Alex rested on the battlements, staring out at the lake.

What was he supposed to do? Who was he supposed to tell about this? Mrs. Hostache? That would surely go well. His father?

His father would think he was insane, that Alex had started building an elaborate fantasy life based on his own name. Wasn't that why he'd been sent away? *Was* he losing it?

No, no. He wasn't insane. He couldn't be.

He should get back inside, but for now he rested, his breath still ragged. Walking slowly along the battlements, he felt like a sentry—a sentry against invading armies and an apparently unlimited supply of hood-wearing tiger women.

Down below, he heard a garage door open.

Off to the left came the creak of wood and metal, very slowly, as if whoever was moving didn't want to be heard. Alex couldn't see the garage door, but he knew where it was, had seen it on the day he moved in. Presently he spied a figure emerging from the darkness, moving through the trees. It was a man, tall and clad in black, headed for a narrow, little-used gate in the stone wall that surrounded the school. A stray beam of light from a lamp on the grounds flashed briefly across him, and Alex recognized the man instantly. It was Mr. Sangster.

As the teacher approached the gate, Alex realized someone else was standing in the darkness on the other side. He strained to hear, moving along the battlements until he was directly over the garage and across from Mr. Sangster. Alex dared to lean over the stone.

Twenty yards away he heard Sangster say something: "What have you got for me?"

"It's Icemaker," came a second voice, female. The dark silhouette through the gate was a woman. Then Alex made out a second word: "Byron."

Byron? *What in the world?*

Alex tried to lean forward some more, straining to hear. "Icemaker," he heard again.

He caught snatches and it was impossible to make sense of it:

The woman was talking. "We think . . . the *Wayfarer*."

". . . sure?"

"Have you . . . entrance of the Scholomance?"

"Not yet," Mr. Sangster said. Alex tried to remember the key words. *Wayfarer. Skolomanse?*

". . . Step it up," said the woman. ". . . catastrophe. . . . In Parma."

Parma. That was a city in Italy. Alex had been there with his family.

She went on but most of it remained lost in the distance. ". . . hasn't come out of hiding in years."

Alex heard Sangster's response clearly. "He's up to something. And he's coming here."

Alex felt a piece of the rock under his elbow give and fall, skittering like gravel down the wall. Sangster looked up sharply and Alex dived. He crouched low and hurried for the entrance back into the hallway. Within seconds, he was in the quaint surroundings of the house.

All the way back to his room, Alex rewound what he had heard below.

Icemaker. Coming here. Catastrophe. And in the middle of it: Sangster.

What. Is going. On.

CHAPTER 5

Friday arrived with a tension in the air that Alex could feel in every step. When he rose, the Merrills were already up and gone. There were no threats. But as he moved through the hall, Alex saw every eye glance toward him, saw whispers between the boys at breakfast. *Secheron*.

In the refectory, Paul and Sid motioned him toward them. Alex slid into one of the squat wooden chairs and put his tray on the table.

"Don't look now, mate," said Paul, "but you're being watched."

Alex took a sip of his orange juice and glanced up. Merrill & Merrill were standing at the far side of the room, waiting for him to make eye contact.

Alex managed a smirk. "They do that at night, too."

"People are nervous," said Sid, who was sketching yet another Scarlet World character. This one wore a doublet and had the bearing of a nobleman.

"Who?" Alex asked.

"Everyone." Alex saw that Sid had given the doublet-wearing vampire a title: The Poet. Sid continued, "People are dropping things more this morning. Two people dropped their trays. Forks are clattering. Everyone's nervous."

"Yeah," Alex said, distracted.

"You're nervous," Paul said, not asking.

"I just got here," Alex said. "This feels so out of control." He was envisioning another meeting between his father and a disgusted headmaster. Then again, if Alex didn't fight back, he could be in real danger. He could see that in Bill's eyes. And the whole school was interested—that would be highly motivating for a crowd-pleaser like Bill. Motivation could really bring out the psycho in a guy. But Bill was asking for trouble. If only he knew.

"How are you getting to Secheron?" Paul asked.

Alex was now watching another table, where several boys were whispering, glancing toward him. "Is there a bus?"

"There's a bus, but it's more fun if you go by bike."

"I don't have a bike." Alex frowned, picking at his eggs. His stomach felt tight and solid. He felt his chest tighten, a sudden rush of nervousness that spread out through his body and tingled at his limbs. He swallowed, washing the feeling down for a moment with orange juice.

"I have an old bike locked up next to the one I got for my birthday," Sid said. "It's not small or anything; I just wanted one with better shocks."

"There, you can take Sid's," said Paul. "You'll love the ride."

Well, that settled that. Alex looked back at the door. The Merrills were gone. "What about the rest of the school—do they want me to get creamed?"

Paul chewed on a piece of toast. He shrugged. "We don't."

"There's ice cream," offered Sid.

After breakfast the tension only grew. Incessant murmurs seemed to throb through some invisible Glenarvon network, *Fight this afternoon fight this afternoon Secheron fight fight.* Alex was envisioning the Merrills pounding his head into the pavement when Mr. Sangster entered the room.

The teacher whom Alex had seen sneak out shortly before two A.M. on Thursday strode into the class wearing a black sweater and dark blue jeans, and for the first time Alex truly studied the man. For one thing, and you wouldn't notice it when he was wearing a jacket, Mr. Sangster was insanely fit. Not built like Arnold Schwarzenegger or anything, but fit as an Olympic swimmer, utterly without fat and narrow at the hips, with well-developed, cordlike arms and chest. Alex watched Mr. Sangster begin to speak while he mentally replayed the bizarre conversation of the night before. Who *was* that at the gate? A girlfriend? *They meet at the gate and speak nonsense?*

Someone handed Bill Merrill a note and Bill took the paper, unfolded it, and read. He smirked, looking back at Alex. The rush of adrenaline shot through Alex again.

"What's that?" Mr. Sangster asked, interrupting his description of the state of science at the time *Frankenstein* was written. The teacher looked at Bill, and Bill shrugged. Mr. Sangster stepped over and snapped up the note. He peered at it as he walked to the front of the class, then laid it on his desk.

Mr. Sangster leaned on the desk for a moment, touching his lip with his thumb. He scanned the room, locked eyes on Alex for a second, and moved on. "No notes," he said.

Class went by in a flash—the minutes warping by as Alex tried to concentrate, flying forward, relentlessly carrying him toward Secheron.

He rose as class ended, having absorbed nothing. He made his way to the front, daring to peek at the note still on Mr. Sangster's desk as the teacher erased the writings on the board that Alex had not bothered to copy down.

On the paper was a picture of Alex—he could tell by the crazy, black locks of hair—and a puddle of something that could have been blood, could have been urine, encircling him as he kneeled in the street.

"What's going on?" asked Mr. Sangster, not looking away from the board.

"Nothing."

Mr. Sangster turned, raised an eyebrow. "It's never nothing, Van Helsing," he said.

It occurred to Alex that Mr. Sangster could stop the whole thing. He might even know the whole plan about the fight already. He had to—every boy in the school was planning to caravan to Secheron after classes were out; by now every teacher had to know. Mr. Sangster could stop it.

But if he wouldn't stop it on his own, Alex would have to ask. And he was being given a chance to do that now.

Mr. Sangster was loading books into an attaché. "I trust the family has taught you to take care of yourself," he said.

Alex stared. "I'm sorry?"

Mr. Sangster looked up and studied Alex for a long moment. He seemed to be trying to suss out whether Alex were telling the truth about something, as if Alex had been asked a question. What did he mean, the family taught him?

"Use what you've learned," Mr. Sangster said. Then he snapped shut his case and walked out, slapping the note against Alex's chest as he went.

The end of the day roared toward him and arrived, and Paul and Sid were there outside the school, leading him to the bike rack.

There were dozens of students on the move, many of them headed for the bus, some on bikes. Alex had no idea where Bill was.

Alex, Paul, and Sid rode in silence down the paved road to Secheron village. Alex wobbled as he rode, his legs made of jelly. He could not have described the bike if he had wanted to. He was remembering something almost exactly like this that had happened before, and he ached to stop it.

Secheron's town square was a picture of Swiss loveliness, with a grand clock rising above an old church, bookstores, and the ice-cream shop open and inviting to the crowd that had already gathered. As Alex parked

Sid's old bike next to some twenty others at the bike rack, he realized the square had formed into a boxing ring. He also noticed that there was an emergency clinic across the square. *Convenient.*

The boys of Glenarvon were bouncing with excitement and Alex could see heads turning in the crowd toward him. Incongruously, tourists still moved about the square. Beyond the gathered boys, three uniformed school girls—there were girls in Switzerland!—sat at an iron table outside the ice-cream parlor working on homework. All of this Alex took in until he permitted himself to move his eyes to the ring, the clearing in the square. Bill Merrill waited, wearing a black T-shirt and a pair of fingerless leather weight gloves. The absurdity of the gloves and the ugliness of the protection they gave, the extra damage Bill's knuckles could do wrapped in leather, filled Alex with more disgust than fear. At his side, Paul and Sid tensed up. "Easy," muttered Paul.

Somewhere through the dread he felt, Alex found the strength to move, stepping forward, the boys parting for him. *Fight. Fight. Fight!* The chant began, the boys winding themselves up, visibly churning their fists, and Alex realized how much they were all animals. It didn't matter whether he was new or not, or whether they liked him or not. They wanted a fight. "You ready?" Bill said, and he stepped forward, bouncing. Alex couldn't will his legs to move, and he saw Paul edging toward the inside of the circle. *No, I'm not ready. This is crazy. You just want me out of your room? Is that all? You're gonna get us kicked out of school!*

Then Alex saw Steven Merrill sucker-punch Paul in the side of the head, taking the big boy down, jumping on top of him. And while Alex was watching Steven and Paul, Bill attacked.

All chants, all bouncing spectators disappeared as Bill's gloved right fist smacked hard against the side of Alex's head. Alex spun, buckling, and they were alone, as if in darkness and lit only by a spotlight that shone on just the two of them. Alex reeled with pain and tried to swing, but Bill was coming forward, throwing him to the ground. Alex felt his shoulders take the brunt of the fall, and his sides were shooting with pain as he realized Bill was landing blow after blow.

For a moment he allowed his hesitation to remain. He wasn't going to do this again. Surely he could figure a way forward in which he didn't have to give this boy what he deserved.

And then he balled up his fists. *Let's go.*

Bill gave a sharp scream and Alex realized he had closed his eyes. He opened them and saw that someone had Bill by the ear, green nails drawing blood as they yanked against the lobe and cartilage. Alex's eyes focused and refocused, his contacts swimming. He scrambled up and saw the new attacker dragging Bill back.

The attacker was a girl, about Alex's age and height, with olive skin and shoulder-length brown hair. Vaguely Alex realized she was one of the girls from the ice-cream parlor. As Bill staggered back, stunned, she let him go and dropped back. Alex could barely take in how she pivoted on her front foot and spun, driving her other foot hard into Bill's chest. Bill sprawled back and flopped into some of the spectators.

Paul was up on his feet now, behind the girl. He had scratches on his face and neck, and Steven was staggering, clutching a bloodied nose. Bill stared in wonder, clutching his bleeding ear.

"What is *this*?" Bill screamed. "Your girlfriend is fighting for you?"

Alex's heart was pounding. *I don't know her,* he wanted to say, as if that would make a difference.

"Get out of here," the girl snarled at Bill as if she were addressing a dog. "Get on out."

Bill seemed to size up the situation. The energy of the crowd had flowed out with the burst of violence and now his moment was gone. Bill nodded sarcastically, pointing at Alex as he backed away, as if to say something meaningful but not finding sufficiently nasty words.

And like that, with a ghostly passing, the lusty energy and the crowd dispersed.

Alex was still breathing hard, staring at Bill and Steven as they got on their bikes and pedaled away. He felt his fists relaxing. Nothing he had predicted had happened. He had looked down the chessboard, made his decision, and then someone had come and kicked the board off the table. He turned to see the girl, who stood like a character in a Japanese cartoon, her arms folded.

"Idiots," she said.

He searched for words. "Who are you?"

The girl looked at Alex, and Paul and Sid, who had gathered to gawk.

"Minnie, with an *h*," she said with a sudden brightness. She waved her hand. "Want some ice cream?"

As Minnie-with-an-h found a table where they could sit, Alex watched her—the way she marched up to the counter and grabbed a handful of menus with cheery but aggressive confidence, the way she immediately started grilling the three of them.

"So is this something you have planned for every Friday, or was it just a limited engagement?" she asked after they ordered sundaes.

"Whuh? Oh," Alex said.

"Our friend Alex here is a pain in the behind to the wrong people," Paul said. "I'm Paul—this is Sid. You said your name was Minnie?"

"M-i-n-h-i. Minhi. So that's Hindu, rather than Mouse." Minhi spoke in perfect idiomatic American English, and yet underneath lay the subtlest hint of an Indian accent that Alex found entrancing. At that moment he would have been glad to ask her to read from the phone book. "Are you from Secheron?" he asked.

Minhi shook her head. "Is anyone? I'm actually from Mumbai. I'm a student at LaLaurie School," she said, tilting her head in the general direction of Lake Geneva. "It's a girls' school across the lake from you guys. So were those like the school bullies or something?"

Alex grimaced at the word *bullies*; it sounded like something out of a film they made you watch in the cafeteria. "Actually, they're my roommates."

The sundaes came, and they tore into them greedily.

Alex continued, "In all fairness, I did ask to be transferred to another room."

"They make his life hell—and this is just a week in," Paul added. "Tell her."

"Tell me what?"

"I . . ." Alex shook his head, embarrassed. "You know, broken alarm clocks, tripping, leaving some . . . really unpleasant stuff in my bed."

"Eww," said Minhi. "So you can't move out?"

"Apparently it's *complicated*," Alex said, thinking of Otranto.

Minhi had laid her bag on the table and Sid spied something. "Are those manga?"

"Yeah." She grew a little red at the temples. "Yeah, I read about three a week."

"What are you on right now?" He was visibly aching to see the books, which Minhi ably recognized. She handed them over.

"Mostly shojo," she said.

Alex nodded. "Shojo, that would be girl comics, right?"

She raised her eyebrows. "What does that mean?"

He smiled. "I mean the lead is a spunky, spiky-haired girl with big eyes. Also there are a lot of hearts. Sometimes everyone has magical powers."

"Way to diss my manga," she said, squinting at him.

"I'm not dissing; I have four sisters, so I've read like a million of them."

"I didn't know that about you," said Paul.

Alex shrugged. He was feeling better. Maybe it would

work out. He hadn't been creamed—and he hadn't done anything crazy, after all.

As though Alex had said his thought aloud, Paul cleared his throat. "So," he said, looking at Alex. "Why *did* you leave your old school?"

Alex took a moment. The Merrills could think anything they wanted, but he actually cared how Sid and Paul felt—they were the closest thing he had to friends so far. Probably it could stay that way. And here was another one, Minhi, who he could already tell was one of the coolest people he'd ever met. And in the next sentence he could blow it, feel them move away from him from there on out. But he wanted to tell the truth.

"I was kicked out," Alex said finally. "I was asked to leave."

The three others shifted, listening. Sid asked, "Why?"

"I got into a fight," Alex said plainly. "It went pretty bad."

Paul wrinkled his brow. "I thought you said you couldn't fight."

Alex looked down. "He was a . . . yeah, a bully. Pretty much like these guys. They're all the same guy." He replayed it briefly in his head. There wasn't much to tell, not that he remembered clearly. He had started feeling snippy and paranoid, had even confided in his father about the paranoia, but in the end he had been cornered one night and snapped. It had been as shocking and frightening to him as to everyone else. "But that one went to the hospital."

Minhi churned at her ice cream. "So you *could* have protected yourself."

"Well," Alex said, embarrassed, trying to change the subject, "if I *had*, we wouldn't have met you."

They sat in silence for a second, and then Paul spoke. Alex could not have been more grateful. "So, Minhi. Where did *you* learn to fight?"

Before Minhi could answer, Alex heard a noise and looked up.

Paul followed Alex's eyes, saying, "What is that?"

The looping sound of a Swiss ambulance filled the air. Within moments a couple of police motorcycles and a white van tore in from the main road, scattering pigeons as they shot across the square to the clinic.

Alex was rising. He thought he knew what this was.

"They're bringing someone in," he heard Minhi say. Alex left the table area and moved across the square almost against his will as a crowd began to gather. He heard whispers from the bystanders: *Another one. Another one.*

Alex stopped at the wall next to the clinic entrance as

two men in white wheeled a gurney to the van, yanking open the vehicle doors. Inside the van was a stretcher covered in a sheet. Another man in white ran back from the van and helped.

Alex wanted to look away, but something urged him to watch as they slid the stretcher out and onto the gurney.

He could see nothing of the person underneath until the gurney jolted over a bump in the entryway.

Drained, completely drained, the man from the ambulance was saying in French.

For a moment the patient's arm, delicate and female, fell down from under the sheet. One of the orderlies reached down and slipped it back in. Within seconds, they had all disappeared into the clinic.

The person's arm had been white as bone.

Alex closed his eyes and turned away finally. When he opened them, Paul and Sid and Minhi were there.

"You don't need to be seeing this stuff," Minhi said. "*We* don't."

Alex composed himself. He nodded, and they all stood around for a moment.

Paul looked up at the clock tower. "We need to get back."

"No kidding," Minhi said. "With all this . . . with the

attacks around the lake, they don't really like us going out at night."

Alex felt depressed and sickened. *Why did I barge over here?*

"Look," Minhi was saying, changing the subject.

She pulled a notebook and pen out of her bag and started writing something. "This is my address at the school, and this is my email—okay? We should get ice cream again sometime when there's, you know, not a fight."

She tore out the sheet and stuck it in a manga. Paul took the book with a smile. "We thank you."

She slung her bag over her shoulder. "You guys be safe."

They watched her go. Paul was clearly impressed by Minhi. The unpleasantness of the ambulance had passed from his mind completely. "All told, mate, this was a fantastic afternoon. But no kidding, we gotta hustle."

Then Alex remembered his roommates. "They're going to be waiting for me."

"Forget it," said Paul, glancing at Sid.

"What?"

"Forget going back there. I don't care what Otranto says, from here on out you're bunking in our room."

CHAPTER 6

Unlike Bill and Steven, Paul and Sid did not have a three-man room. Theirs was smaller: smaller window, smaller shelves, smaller bathroom, and with only one bunk set, so they had to make out a pallet for Alex on the floor.

It was perfect.

As they prepared for bed, Alex wondered if the Merrills would report him, but then he realized they were unlikely to—they were still bruised and now they would have to answer questions. Besides, they wanted the room to themselves.

"You can go back in the daytime tomorrow and collect your stuff. I hope you don't have much," joked Paul as he handed over some extra sheets and towels that had been in the closet. *Yeah, 'cause the Merrills will probably destroy it,* Alex thought.

"Not much," he said, folding some extra blankets to make a pillow.

"Didn't leave like a Nintendo or something?"

"I *wish*." Alex shook his head. No video games were allowed at Glenarvon. Alex went to the sink in the bathroom and took out his contacts, emerging with his glasses on.

Alex on the floor, Paul and Sid on the bunks—lights out and they went to sleep, and Alex slept like a baby.

Until one thirty.

Alex must have been subconsciously listening for the sound of the garage door, because he was lost in a strange dream of the woman in white who fell to dust, and then came the gravelly roll of the garage door, far below. Alex blinked awake.

He grabbed his glasses and rose, pulling on his clothes and, this time, shoes. Downstairs and outside in seconds.

Huddling close to the school walls, Alex saw Sangster pushing a motorcycle across the yard toward the gate, moving faster than seemed possible as he walked the large machine on its sparkling wheels.

As he hustled around the building, Alex could hear the motorcycle starting. He rushed to the bike rack for Sid's extra bike, unchaining it and hopping on. He headed for the road, listening for the sound of Sangster's much faster machine. He wouldn't be able to keep up with the instructor, obviously, but the roads were long and he might get lucky.

Sangster seemed to be headed for Secheron. Even with the muffling trees lining the winding road, Alex could see and hear the motorcycle ahead for a longer time than he expected. Then, after a few minutes, the noise was too far away.

But it was lovely on the road at night—the sound of frogs and owls and the gentle creak of the bicycle. He would head back into the tiny town and ride around, see if he could spot the motorcycle parked outside somewhere. It was a mission of curiosity, but he was so transfixed by the beauty of the ride that he realized he didn't care whether he learned anything or not. *Why does Sangster sneak out at night? Well, why do I?*

Then his head filled with static and warning—quiet at first but building more rapidly than it ever had. In less than a minute the pitch inside his mind became almost deafening.

Ice-cold air shot down the road from behind and

enveloped him, a cold front dropping in so suddenly that Alex nearly fell over as his muscles tensed. His breath became visible as he kept pedaling. Then he became aware of a rumbling that he felt in his bones, vibrating up from the road and through his feet.

He heard what he thought was Sangster, a motorcycle engine's roar, but then realized it was coming from behind, from the other direction.

The sound grew louder and Alex stopped, putting down his legs and standing on the bike at the side of the road, just around a curve.

He heard three, four, maybe even six motorcycles. There were no headlights visible anywhere. But they were coming fast.

Black shapes tore around the bend. Two motorcycles roared toward Alex, ridden by men in dark red clothes and face covers. Realizing he was still partly in the road, Alex dragged the bike off the shoulder, dropping it as he scrambled to crouch behind some bushes. The rumble was now insanely loud, and two motorcycles shot past, giving way to four, and then eight.

And more. Blasts of icy air seemed to roll with the engines' roar. Then came trucks, armored personnel carriers, and modified Humvees, followed by more motorcycles, then SUVs, and more bikes. Some of the vehicles had open sides, and there were dark-clad figures riding in them.

This would be one of those things that don't happen.

Some three hundred meters away, on a tower built for observing fires, the man called Sangster brought a pair of infrared glasses up to his eyes. "I've got the caravan. They're on the road to Secheron," he said into the mike on his earpiece. Through the binoculars, the shapes on the vehicles on the road shone a brilliant, icy blue. He could make out the cold shapes of trees, a few woodland creatures—and there, an orange-and-red form, hunkered down next to the road.

"Guys, this is Sangster; do we have a second agent by the road?"

After a moment a voice came online. "Negative, we have no other operatives on this task."

Sangster snarled in disgust. "There's a human watching."

The voice crackled on the radio. "Watching? Have they spotted him yet?"

"Doesn't look like it." Sangster chewed his lip. "Should I engage?"

"Negative, stay on task."

"Copy," Sangster replied, but he was already off task.

He moved in closer, trying to get a better look. He put on a pair of modified sunglasses, adjusted them for darkness and magnification, and looked for a clear view of the bystander.

The caravan was still moving, but Sangster adjusted his glasses back at the shape on the side of the road. The person was not a journalist: He didn't hunker down the way an experienced man would. He or she crouched. Sangster allowed that given the shorter height of the figure, it could be a female.

Flicker of light—a reflector. The figure had a bicycle.

"It's a kid," Sangster said, aghast.

"Stay on task."

The static in Alex's head pounded now, and he clutched his head and stared, astonished at the size of the caravan. His brain swirled with thoughts of what in the world this could be—UN peacekeepers? A night invasion of Switzerland? What on earth lay on the road around Lake Geneva that would bring such an army? And why no lights?

And as he stayed down behind the bush, daring to stick his head out, *Why the freaking cold?*

Alex bumped into the bike with his shin as he shifted his weight, barely noticing the flicker of light that shot off the front reflector as the wheel adjusted.

On the caravan, peering out the door of a personnel carrier, a figure, bald and tall in an oxblood red leather jacket, turned his head as the flicker of the bike's reflector shone next to the road. The bald man frowned and touched a button on an electronic device strapped to his wrist.

Alex watched as the caravan slowed a bit. Out of instinct he began to back up, crablike in his crouch. There was a Humvee opposite him in the road, and suddenly the black tarp that stretched across it shot back.

Two red-clad figures leapt from the vehicle. Alex took just a moment to watch them landing on their feet—just a moment to see they bore no weapons, but that as they opened their mouths to hiss, he saw enormous fangs.

Run. Get out. Run. Alex sprang out of his crouch and into a sprint, leaping over Sid's bike and hurtling deeper into the woods. He didn't look to see if they were coming, but somewhere in the cold air he swore he could hear them laughing.

His luck was about to run out. He had twice faced just *one* such creature and barely survived. This was way beyond hurling clay tiles, sticks, and weather vanes.

He ran, not looking back until a moment when he paused by a tree. *Maybe they didn't see me. Maybe the two in the street just stopped to look around. Or relieve themselves. Or hiss at the moon.*

Through the trees he saw the shapes moving, leaping, and not just two.

They were coming for him.

Alex started to run again but suddenly they were there, within fifty yards and closing in. One of them leapt and landed in front of him, slamming to the ground, leaves flying.

The vampire—male, long and slender in his red commando outfit—bent toward Alex and hissed.

At that instant there was a rapid staccato sound that tore through the air. The creature was still hissing as it burst into flame and turned to dust with a sharp, crackling sound.

There was another motorcycle roaring toward Alex, coming in fast from the side. Dirt and moss kicked up as the bike ground to a halt between him and the rest of the vampires.

Sangster—*Mr.* Sangster, his literature teacher—was still wearing his jeans and sweater, but had added a pair of silver-and-black, many-buttoned goggles, a Bluetooth device at his ear, and an assault rifle to the mix.

Sangster held out his hand. "Get on, Alex," he said. He turned and shot at two more of the vampires. The gun made a violent, heavy sound, *buddabuddabudda.* "Get on!"

Alex's head spun with a thousand questions but none of them would be answered if he died right here. He grabbed Sangster's hand, swinging himself up onto the back of the bike. Sangster put Alex's arms around his waist, and they were off like a shot.

"There are more of them coming," Sangster shouted, tapping at a rearview mirror, and Alex saw with astonishment that it was not an actual mirror but a screen displaying infrared images. In the infrared, he could see the creatures leaping like jaguars behind the bike, each one a brilliant image of icy blue light.

"Put these on." Sangster fished a second pair of goggles out of a satchel near his thigh. Alex clenched his knees together on the bike and took them. He struggled for a moment to pull the rubber strap over the back of his head, bringing the goggles to rest over his own glasses.

Suddenly, the whole world was in the negative, the trees brilliant white against a gray background. Alex tried to follow the path of the bike, barely able to keep his eyes open as Sangster tore through and over bushes, somehow managing to dodge trees. The double glasses violently wobbled on his ears. "I'm sorry!" he was shouting before he even realized it. "I'm sorry, I shouldn't have gone out!"

"Don't worry about that now," Sangster yelled over

the roar. "Hit the button next to your left eyebrow."

Alex took a moment, his arm jolting. *Breathe.* He found the button and pressed.

"This way you can hear me," Sangster said, and Alex heard the voice, gyrating through the bones of his own head, muffled but audible.

"Where are we going?" Alex asked.

He heard Sangster's voice over the engine's roar. "Someplace safe."

CHAPTER 7

Sangster seemed to be aiming for the spaces between the trees as though he were skiing. Alex dared to look again in the infrared. The vampires were still in pursuit.

"They're coming after us because they want that caravan kept secret," said Sangster, almost casually considering the danger at hand. "We're close to HQ. Maybe we can lose them."

Sangster reached up, tapped a button on his glasses, and now in Alex's goggle vision—surely also through Sangster's—a GPS map appeared. The image displayed over the view in front of him, so that the map bounced amid the trees.

"Farmhouse," Sangster said, swerving hard to avoid a branch. The vampires' shapes were leaping closer.

"Please repeat your request," came a singsong sound response.

"FARM-HOUSE."

The GPS view before Alex's eyes shifted. First it showed one location, which it indicated with the symbol of a little roofed house, and then the camera rose up into the sky and located the motorcycle moving through the woods. Then the GPS drew a line between the two: their path.

"That's two miles away." Sangster adjusted his course, heading north. "But we're gonna have a problem."

"What?" Alex asked, incredulous. *Vampires chasing us isn't problem enough?*

Sangster was already speaking rapidly into his mike to someone else. "This is Agent Sangster requesting permission to enter Farmhouse accompanied by non-cleared human."

A voice came on the line. "Could you repeat . . . ?"

"I have a kid with me, I need in," Sangster said, swerving again, barely able to speak with the bounce of the motorcycle.

"Denied."

"I cannot—"

"If you enter the perimeter of Farmhouse with a non-cleared witness, you will be shot."

Alex saw Sangster glance up at the trees. For a split second Alex glimpsed metallic gray cameras, recessed against the firs. The cameras swiveled as they passed. "We're coming up on the perimeter," Sangster said.

Alex looked ahead and saw a tree line coming up fast, a large clearing in the woods, with a small, dilapidated farmhouse a hundred yards beyond, a distant white image bouncing behind the trees.

They were running out of woods. Alex felt the bike brake hard on its front wheel. He was weightless for a second as the rear of the bike lifted off the forest floor, swinging violently around as Sangster ground the bike to a halt. The motorcycle dropped back down and they were facing the pursuers now. Alex noticed that Sangster was shifting his weight to guard him. Sangster started firing the rifle he carried.

Buddabuddabudda. Alex counted seven, maybe eight vampires ripping through the trees.

"Requesting permission to enter with—"

"Negative, that witness was to be left. Leave him and report; we cannot have—"

"Dammit, he's a Van Helsing," Sangster hissed. Alex

turned, startled, and looked at him.

Silence on the other end of the line. Sangster tagged one of the vampires in the head, sending it spinning as it burned and dusted. They were landing close, baring their fangs. And now Alex realized he had miscounted— as these eight drew closer, he saw three or four more ice blue cold shapes in the woods.

Suddenly one of the vamps was hit in the head by a round Sangster didn't fire, a single shot from somewhere at the house.

The radio crackled. "Granted."

Sangster shouted, "We're in," and the bike leapt, spinning once more and hurtling again through the trees and into the clearing with the vampires close behind. Alex felt the bike pick up speed as they moved onto the smooth grass. They were hurtling straight for the tin wall of a small shack next to the house.

Alex winced as a hot electric pulse shot through his headset.

"We're blowing out electronic communications," shouted Sangster. "Just in case those guys are miked. We can't let them report a thing."

Another shot rang out from somewhere Alex couldn't see and Sangster said, "This perimeter has to be a dead zone."

They were ten yards from the wall of the shack.

Five yards and the side of the shack whipped up with a metallic roar, nearly catching the bike's front wheel. Sangster gunned the engine and Alex held on tight as they drove under the rising wall and began zooming down a long concrete drive.

The bike roared down the grade and commandos ran up, ten or twenty men and women. Alex looked back for a second, and saw the muzzle of a blond woman's weapon flashing. She left the tunnel, already firing, laying waste to the vampires in the clearing. For a moment she was silhouetted against the floodlights of the farmhouse clearing as Alex and Sangster moved farther and farther below, then Alex turned his head back to the front.

Down, down into the bowels of the earth they sped, past wooden beams and newer, iron girders, down a full half mile at a 30-degree angle until the motorcycle slowed. They reached a vast, concrete expanse lit by high tracks of lighting. It was an enormous bunker under the woods.

Alex felt his eyes grow wide as he took in countless vehicles, Humvees and trucks and even helicopters.

A man in a suit—older, with a slight paunch—was waiting for them when the bike rolled to a stop. As Alex slid off the bike and removed the goggles, the man folded his arms.

"Alexander Van Helsing. Son of Charles and Amanda. Whatever are we going to do with you?"

CHAPTER 8

"How do you know who I am?" said Alex, coming to stand on legs that, he was proud to note, were only slightly shaky. "And what is this?" He looked around at the vehicles, noticing that at the end of the "garage" was a set of metal staircases leading up into doors in the rock wall. He had no way of guessing how much more space there might be on the other side of the doors.

He looked back at the ramp they'd come down as the contingent of commandos returned with the heavy, staccato sound of boots on concrete.

"Did you get them all?" Sangster asked.

"We got those around the perimeter," replied the woman Alex had seen as they'd come through the door.

She strode up and laid down her weapon on a table with a number of other rifles like it. The woman was about half a head shorter than Sangster but all muscle, with shoulder-length, dirty-blond hair and a healthy smattering of freckles. "But you gotta figure one or two made it back to the caravan."

The older man in the suit frowned. "Either way, the caravan will surely be intrigued that they sent a handful of vampires to kill a human witness and the party never returned." He was watching Alex now, running his eyes up and down. "Let's not talk here," he said, looking around. Besides the commandos, there was a lot of activity in the garage, crews working on vehicles and milling about.

Sangster nodded and they all began to move up a flight of metal stairs to a door. Sangster and the woman kept Alex between them as they came through the door and into a carpeted foyer of the kind you'd find in an office building. They moved swiftly, Alex silently taking it all in as they walked past rooms that even at this late hour were filled with men and women busy at workstations, studying dots on massive maps displayed on glass walls.

They filed into a conference room and Sangster indicated a chair halfway down the length of the table. Alex took it. Sangster sat across, with the woman at Sangster's right and the older man at the head.

Alex leaned in for a closer look at the long, black table. There were computer screens inlaid in its slick surface. In the center of the table was a sort of crest or shield, a circular symbol that bore a Latin phrase: *Talia sunt.* Below that a single word:

"'Polidorium,'" Alex read aloud. He looked up. "Who *are* you people?"

The older man gestured at the other two. "This is Agent Armstrong," he said, and the blond, freckled woman nodded, not smiling. "You've met Agent Sangster. My name is Carerras." He turned to Sangster. "Do his parents know he's here?"

Sangster shook his head. "He must have snuck out; I think he followed me."

"We have to decide what to tell the Van Helsings."

"Hang on," Alex interrupted, infuriated. "*Stop*. What do you mean, what to tell the Van Helsings—I'm sorry, I—what is this? I mean, those were—those things on the road were . . ."

"Technically, modified post-initial-failure humans," said Sangster. "Vampires. What, you've never seen them before?"

Alex paused. He came to a decision. "No, actually

I'm starting to see them a lot. I saw one in the woods. It attacked me. I killed it."

"Really? How did you kill it?"

"Luck," Alex said tiredly. "Luck. Those things aren't supposed to exist. And then there was another one."

"Where?"

"The school. It was outside my window, looking in at me. It chased me across the roof."

Sangster folded his arms. "Hmmm." Alex's eyes fell again on the crest on the table and he thought back to the snatches of conversation he'd caught at the gate. "What is the Polidorium?"

"I can't believe you don't know," Sangster said. After a moment, looking at Carerras and Armstrong, Sangster went on, "*We* are the Polidorium. Founded by Dr. John Polidori in 1821."

"John Polidori?" Alex asked, thinking of the introduction to *Frankenstein* and the notes about it. "The guy from the Frankenstein party?"

Armstrong ran her fingers through her hair. Even across the table, Armstrong and Sangster still smelled like gunpowder, and it suddenly made Alex feel like heaving. "We like to think of it as the Polidori party," said Armstrong.

"So," said Carerras, pulling out a pouch and a pipe.

As he began to prepare his pipe he summed it up. "You don't know much about vampires, or about us. What can you tell us about *you*?"

Alex looked up. "What do you mean?"

"How old are you? Where did you live before now? And if you're not up on *us*, what do you know about the Van Helsing Foundation?"

Alex spoke slowly, wondering this time if the truth were the right answer. He told it anyway. "I'm fourteen, and my parents and my sisters live in Wyoming right now. The Van Helsing Foundation, that's a charitable organization my dad runs as chairman."

"Wait a second." Armstrong leaned forward, taking Alex's glasses off his face in a quick swipe. She held them up to the light, studying them.

"Hey, I need those," Alex protested. She was a blur now. He couldn't even make out her face, and the sudden blindness made him feel trapped and claustrophobic.

"He doesn't wear those in class," Sangster said. "I've never seen you wear glasses."

"I wear *contacts*," Alex snapped.

Armstrong was still peering intently at the pair of glasses. "Why aren't you wearing contacts now?"

"It's like three A.M.!" he said.

Armstrong pursed her lips, then handed them back. "They're normal," she said, satisfied. Alex put the glasses back on, very slowly.

Carerras spoke. "You're aware, no doubt, of the associations of your family name?"

Alex chewed on this, on the absurdity of all of this, the G.I. Joe figures studying his glasses as though they might be made of kryptonite, a man in a suit a mile underground asking this or any question in the middle of the night. "You mean, 'vampire hunter'? Like in the movies? There are worse names to have," Alex said. "But yes, I hear a *lot* about it. My dad gets annoyed every time someone even mentions that character. It's like running around with the name Hannibal."

Sangster shook his head in something like wonder and addressed the others. "I did some research when I saw his name on my roster of students. He climbs mountains. He rescues hikers. He's been taught to survive on little or no rest or food. He can drive a combine and ride a motorbike, and he once survived a snakebite by applying a tourniquet to his own leg, nearly causing him to lose a foot." Alex felt a tinge of pride and fear as his literature teacher recited a litany of things that, over the years, Alex had indeed been taught to do. His father had encouraged all of his children in these things. Well, not the tourniquet. "And yet *not a single thing* does he know about the one thing he should know most: vampires. He hasn't been trained to fight them. As far as I can tell he knows nothing of the business."

Carerras asked, "Have any of the Van Helsings been active?"

"Charles is inactive. We all know about Amanda," Sangster said, "and—"

"What does *that* mean?" demanded Alex.

Sangster said evenly, "All it means is that without your mother, your father would probably still be on the payroll."

"This is crazy," Alex said, rising and shaking his head.

"Can you give us a minute or two?" Sangster looked at the others.

A moment later Sangster and Alex were alone in the conference room and Sangster was pressing buttons on an invisible keyboard in the table. As a projection screen dropped down from the ceiling, he spoke into the table-top. "Gimme a club soda." He turned to Alex. "You want a Dr Pepper?"

"What are you trying to say about my mother?" Alex said, frowning.

Sangster had an open expression that Alex took to

be one of peacemaking. "Do you want something to drink?" he asked again.

"Whatever."

Sangster made the order and turned his attention to the keyboard. He hit a button and a jagged, infrared image filled the screen on the wall: a man leaping toward a camera on a balcony somewhere as a politician's motorcade rolled in the streets below. The attacker's nails were sharp and his teeth—fangs—were bared.

"We kill vampires, Alex." Sangster hit the button again and now showed another infrared image, a different vampire leaping onto a car in the motorcade, ripping back the windshield like paper. "Guys like us, some of us hunt terrorists; some of us fight wars. The Polidorium was founded to hunt vampires."

"Just vampires?"

"Eh," Sangster said noncommittally. He tapped the invisible keyboard and now brought up an image of a young Italian man in a painting. "This is Polidori."

Alex tried to remember details of the lecture on *Frankenstein*. That all seemed like a year ago. "We talked about him in class. Mary Shelley makes him sound like an idiot. You said that guy seemed like a loser."

"Here is what you must know if we are to go forward," Sangster said seriously. "There are two Polidoris. The one we read about and the one we honor by serving this organization."

Now below the portrait of Polidori appeared two columns—two sets of biographical data points.

The door opened and an agent brought a tray with their drinks. Sangster indicated the Dr Pepper and Alex took it as his mysterious teacher continued.

"According to the accepted literature, John Polidori fell out with his friend Lord Byron in 1816, shortly after they stayed here at Lake Geneva. Broke and depressed, Polidori supposedly died of a drug overdose just a few years later.

"Here is what any agent of the Polidorium will tell you if you have the right to hear it, and God help me, whether your father likes it or not, you do."

As Sangster spoke, he tapped a button and another screen lit up, flashing images: helicopters and motorcycles, machinery and computers, the screens with GPS coordinates of agents moving across the globe.

"John Polidori was not a fool. He *altered* his life, starting after his book, *The Vampyre*, the first modern book on vampires.

"In 1818, as his book was coming out, Polidori faced his first coven of vampires, a group running an opium den in London. He traced those vampires to a clan running a newspaper and a publishing house. He killed several but the vampires began to turn public opinion against the doctor, who was obliged to keep his activities a secret. Polidori soon found his bad reputation useful. By now, he had a mission. He faked his own death and went underground.

"By 1831, when Mary Shelley wrote her revised *Frankenstein*, everyone remembered Polidori as an idiot—Mary included. She even changed her description of what he was writing about—nowhere does she use the word *vampire*; instead she makes up a story about a skull-headed lady.

"But Polidori made friends. Among other people, in the late 1830s he met the young Abraham Van Helsing, who *was* a real person, despite what you've heard. Bram Stoker met him when Van Helsing was an old man and wrote his book *Dracula* based on Van Helsing's story. A long time before that, Van Helsing had used some of his own considerable wealth to help Polidori create this organization. When Polidori did die—in 1851, thirty years *after* his reported death—the Polidori Society stretched across Europe and the United States and was receiving money from the black budgets of every nation. From time to time they continued to work with the Van Helsing Foundation—your father's research foundation."

"The VHF is made up of scholars and doctors," said Alex. "They make malaria vaccines and run clinics in third-world countries. I don't see any of those guys chasing vampires through the woods."

"They do more than that, but the activities you are talking about give them reason to operate across the planet," said Sangster. "And when they need firepower, they call the Polidorium."

Alex stared at the image of the Italian doctor who had worked with his—*what would it be?* "So Abraham Van Helsing was my—"

"Great-great-great-grandfather," said Sangster. "That would be *three* greats."

"Do you know my father?"

"Not personally."

"But he was an—he was what you are."

"He was an agent, yes."

"He never told me any of this," Alex said, and now he flashed on the white-fanged creatures pursuing him through the woods.

And then on something else.

"If you did research on me," Alex asked slowly, "then do you know about . . ."

"About your old school?" Sangster asked calmly, when Alex found that he couldn't complete the sentence. Alex nodded.

Back at Frayling Prep, Alex had felt the jagged static for the first time. At the beginning he had put it down to being away from home at boarding school, the ache of homesickness for the six family members he'd left behind. But then he noticed that the static only seemed to occur in the presence of one fellow classmate, a guy named Max Pierce. Pierce seemed harmless enough—sure, he picked on some of the younger students, but he was nowhere near as mean as Merrill & Merrill, despite what Alex had told Paul, Sid, and Minhi in Secheron earlier that day. But Alex couldn't get over his unease. He'd confided in his father, who told him he probably wasn't getting enough sleep, and that it was just migraines. "They run in the family," his father had said.

And then the incident. Studying late one night in the library, Alex had looked up at the window in time to see a figure hurry out of the chapel on the Frayling campus. At that moment Alex felt that static again, pounding in his brain, driving him out onto the grounds.

He had found Pierce, in a tree, peeping into one of the girl's dorms. Pierce's shoes were off and he was using his toes to balance, and when Alex called out to him, Pierce had swiveled toward him with a lustful, drooling look. It was as though Pierce were possessed by some animal part of himself. Pierce launched himself at Alex.

Pierce hadn't fought like a kid; he fought like a

maniac, clawing and biting. Alex defended himself using the techniques he had been taught—and a quickness of reflex that seemed to come out of nowhere. The fight was brutal and fast, and accompanied by a sound that Alex could only define as "snarling"—animal-like snarling, coming from Pierce's snapping mouth. And at the end of it, Pierce lay there, bleeding from the nose and mouth, unconscious. Horrified at what he had done and unsure of what he had seen, Alex had begun to shudder uncontrollably, and that's when the dean came out of his office on his way to his car and found them.

"Pierce was a werewolf, Alex," Sangster said. He tapped some keys on the keyboard in the table and there Alex's face was on the screen, next to the Frayling expulsion report. And more: a picture of Pierce. No, two pictures. One was Pierce's student ID photo and the other was a photo of a wolflike head with eyes that looked familiar. Pierce's.

"Why do you have this?"

"This entry in the database is on our American servers; it was triggered by an anonymous tip. We can keep an eye on him now. Your fight was in the middle of the lunar cycle—Pierce was itching for a change but wouldn't have undergone a full transformation for another week. During the day he was normal, so no one but you ever noticed."

"The school called my father," Alex said, almost to himself. "He came right away. He was furious. He talked to the counselors and police and got me out with only an expulsion and no jail time, no newspaper stories. I gotta say that I got off easy. But when we were finally alone and I told him what I—what I *felt*, the way Pierce acted, he made me promise not to mention it ever again. He said people would think I was crazy. It even sounded like he thought I *was* crazy. But if what you're saying is true, he probably knew all about it. That Pierce was a werewolf."

Alex couldn't help feeling betrayed by this realization. His father had lied to him, and worse, made him question his own sanity. *How could he—what would be worth that?* "So . . . why didn't he tell me?" Alex asked.

"I don't know why he didn't tell you," said Sangster. "But he's been preparing you. All your life. Self-defense. Mountain rescue. Whether he likes it or not, he knows what you're going to be."

Alex wondered if Dad knew he had spent a considerable part of the past week running for his life. "Who was that on the road tonight?"

"Icemaker," Sangster replied. He tapped at the keys again, and now a new sketch appeared—a cruel-eyed man with swept-back hair. "That was the arriving caravan of a clan lord, a big boss, that we call Icemaker."

"You call him that because of the cold?" Alex asked.

"That's right."

"You give all the vampires cool superhero names?"

Sangster smiled.

Alex went on. "So who is this Icemaker?"

"Polidori knew him as, believe it or not, Lord Byron," Sangster said. The sketch morphed into an older image: The eyes and face remained, but now the hair was longer and the man's clothes were in the ruffled, nineteenth-century style. "The poet . . . and the first vampire Polidori ever faced. That last summer when the whole group of friends was together, the Haunted Summer, is the summer that Byron began to consort with vampires. Byron was an arrogant man, attractive to every woman he met and able to best any man in any contest, but he was plagued by self-consciousness, about his club foot, his height, his reputation as a writer. Vampirism attracts people who want to become something greater than themselves. It took years before Byron became a full vampire, but Polidori saw it coming. Obviously this isn't the kind of thing I would ever teach in class."

Too bad for Sid, Alex thought. Sangster went on.

"Today Icemaker controls thousands of vampire soldiers. He's very secretive, even for a clan lord. But know this: He is extraordinarily dangerous. When he needs blood, he doesn't just come in and kill a few, he kills hundreds. He'll attack, freeze the town, then reduce it to shards."

"Do you know why he's here?" Alex asked.

"Nope. We got word that he destroyed one of our ships, the *Wayfarer*, which had a cargo of relics and other holdings on its way to a warehouse in the States. Then suddenly we started tracking him here. Something got his attention and drove him back to Lake Geneva."

"Where would they be going? Where would they put all of those vehicles?"

"In a place we can't find," Sangster said. "A place even better hidden than this: a place called the Scholomance."

Alex nodded. He had heard that word. "That's a hide-out?"

"It's a school, more a university, like an MIT for vampires."

"And it's around here?"

"We think so," Sangster said. He tapped another key and Alex nearly choked on his drink.

There, in a blurry photograph, was a shot of his own father, that skinny, seldom-exercised man, here twenty years younger, fitter, and hunkered down behind a crumbled wall as he talked on a radio. "Where was this taken?"

Sangster looked up. "Hmmm . . . I'd say Prague."

"*When* was this taken?"

"I would figure not long before you were born." Sangster looked at Alex searchingly. He smiled and then said, "Come *on*, Alex."

"What?"

"One more time: It's *really* your position that you have never heard of the Polidorium or the work it does? And that your knowledge of the Van Helsing Foundation is restricted to its charitable activities?"

"Yes! Everything you said." Alex couldn't take his eyes off the picture. *Incredible. Dad was an honest-to-God, hunkering-down-behind-crumbling-buildings-and-shooting-things spy.* "Doesn't happen," Alex muttered.

"What?"

"All my life my dad brushes off anything that he thinks sounds like nonsense with 'that doesn't happen.' But it turns out that everything that doesn't happen actually does."

"Probably not everything," Sangster said. "Anyway, we can't keep you from talking. Even if we tried, drugs wear off. I have no idea what we're going to do with you."

"Can *I* learn this stuff?" Alex said, stepping closer to the screen.

"Maybe you should ask your dad that," Sangster said, studying Alex.

"I don't get it. Why would he send me here? If he didn't want me involved with this."

"He didn't send you *here*," Sangster responded, "he sent you to one of the most prestigious private schools in the world." The teacher/agent bit his lip. "I don't think he knows the Polidorium has a location at Lake Geneva. It's top secret, and it's only been here since we started focusing our search for the Scholomance. We don't share that kind of information with former agents."

"If you tell him, he'll drag me out of here," Alex said seriously. "That'll be it for me. I don't want that. This is too much to turn my back on."

Sangster rose, tapped a key, and the screen went dark. Then he turned back to Alex with a serious look. "Alex, can you sense them?"

Alex sat silently for a moment. "I think so. When they're close. I felt it the other night in my room."

"At school?"

"Yes, and then it—she—was there, outside my window. And . . . I felt it at Frayling, too."

Sangster was weighing something in his head.

"You tired?"

Alex had to admit he was.

"Let's go back to school. It's going to be morning in a few hours."

They exited the boardroom and Armstrong and Carerras were down by the foyer in conversation.

Sangster went to find a jacket and helmet for Alex. As Alex waited, he watched the other commandos going about their business, putting back their weapons, fooling around.

Armstrong was talking to Carerras, who was puffing away at his pipe. "Still have no idea where they are," Carerras was saying.

"We might have found out tonight."

"Never can tell."

Sangster returned and handed Alex the helmet. "If you felt it the other night before it chased you at the school, then it's worse than I thought," he said.

"What do you mean?"

"They know you're here."

CHAPTER 9

"Up and at 'em, hero," Paul was saying. Alex lay in his makeshift bed, wincing against the light, as Paul and Sid moved about the room, the morning sun streaming in. He blinked awake.

"What?"

Paul was looking in the mirror at the bruise that shone bright blue on the side of his head. "You don't want to miss breakfast this morning," he said. "Everyone is going to be cheering after yesterday."

Alex was confused for a moment and then it all came flooding back. After the woods and the motorcycles and the vampires and the cave, he had completely forgotten that the evening had begun with the Secheron fight. In fact, he had almost gone back to the Merrills' room after Sangster had dropped him off, wordlessly, at the gate.

Alex moved like a zombie through washing up and putting in his contacts as Paul and Sid lingered near the door, ready to go down to the refectory.

Sid was watching him. "You look terrible," he said.

"Maybe it's the sleeping on the floor," Paul said. "I can see if we can add more blankets."

"No, no." Alex waved a hand, his mind still racing through everything he had seen. "No, it's fine." He splashed his face again. His eyes were a little sore, but he was getting better at putting his contacts in. He was thinking of the moment when the creatures had spotted him, as he crouched next to . . . next to Sid's bike.

He slapped his forehead in disgust. "The . . ." He turned around, reaching for his sneakers and jamming his feet into them. "You guys go on."

"What are you doing?" Paul stared.

"I forgot—I wanted to go for a walk. You know . . . think," he said awkwardly.

"You wanted to . . . *think*?" Paul repeated the words as though he had never heard them before. He pointed to the scratches on his face and neck. "People will be cheering. Look at my face! This is like a medal."

Alex smacked Paul on the shoulder as he ran out the

door. "Enjoy it."

He raced down the stairs, past bleary-eyed students on their way to breakfast. Headmaster Otranto was coming in from outside and Alex nearly bumped into him, eliciting a short, disapproving look.

Out the door, onto the path, through the gate, a steady pace to the road. He had forgotten Sid's bike, left it in the woods halfway to Secheron. He was glad for the mistake—he wanted to go back into the woods. Unlike school, the woods were a clearer world, of hooded monsters and agents on motorcycles. Every inch of the area crawled with the kind of energy that he barely felt in his everyday school life. Out here there was energy with purpose. Heroes on a mission. Alex found himself thinking hard as he ran.

The trees looked unfamiliar in the daylight, but after a while he felt he was reaching the bend where he had left the road, where the caravan had started to pass. Finally he saw the glint of the reflector on Sid's bike as it lay in the leaves.

Alex froze. There, leaning against a tree, arms folded, was Sangster, wearing a navy blue jogging suit. "We need to talk," he said.

Alex went to the bike and lifted it. "I want in," he said.

"What do you mean, 'in'?" Sangster asked.

"You showed me pictures of my father. I can do it. I want in."

"Are you sure that's what you need to be doing right now?" Sangster asked. "You're skilled and you're lucky, but I gotta admit, I'm worried that you shouldn't even stay in the area."

"What else am I supposed to do?" Alex asked, and he meant the question sincerely. "Even if I wanted to be normal, to lead a normal life—I've got these vibrations in my head when I see these—oh, wait, right—*monsters*."

"And they know you have that," Sangster said. "I'm willing to bet that the Scholomance got wind that a Van Helsing was in Geneva."

"Last night when you guys were checking out my glasses, you were acting like you thought maybe I was spying on you," said Alex. "Spying for my dad, I guess."

"Right."

"Why would he want me to do that?"

"The relationship is complicated," Sangster said.

"You gotta understand that's just not part of what I know of my father. I want to learn about that. I want to learn to do what he did."

"Alex," Sangster said soothingly, "this stuff takes years to learn. And you *have* years."

"Oh, give me a break," Alex said. Sangster was calling him a kid basically. That was what this was about. Alex was furious. Last night Sangster had sounded ready to hand him a machine gun. "First, I've already killed one of those things without any of your training. And second, I can learn to do what you do. You think I can't ride through *trees*?"

Sangster tilted his head. "I didn't say I don't think it will happen. I already told you that. *Some*day."

Alex started rolling the bike. "I have to go. Paul and Sid are waiting."

"Be careful on these roads," Sangster called, adding to Alex's irritation.

Alex returned the bike and made it to the refectory just as Paul and Sid were getting up from breakfast. Sure enough, there was a crowd of admirers gathered around, who indeed regarded Paul's scratches and wounds as badges of honor. Alex's bruises ran up and down his body but were generally invisible, and he felt a twinge of jealousy.

"How was your walk?" Sid asked. Alex shrugged.

A hand clapped down on his shoulder from behind. Alex spun, anticipating a fanged demon that would bite his head in half. Close enough. It was Bill Merrill.

"You didn't come in last night," Bill said.

Behind Alex, Paul and Sid grew serious. Steven Merrill, nursing his own wounds, lingered nearby.

"I was there," Alex said evenly. "Don't you remember?"

This answer caught Bill by surprise—he was about to respond, then stopped and seemed to chew on it. *Get there faster, Bill,* thought Alex. Bill looked back at Steven, who pursed his lips.

"Yeah," Bill said finally. "Maybe so. But don't think for a minute we're done."

"Okay," Alex said.

Paul made a time-out gesture with his hands. "It's Saturday, mates. Saturday. For the love of God. Let's all do something else."

Bill and Steven consulted each other and reached an agreement. "See you tonight, *roomie,*" said Bill.

"Wouldn't miss it for the world," Alex said, knowing they were glad to be rid of him. He hoped that would be the end of it.

Alex, Paul, and Sid spent the rest of the day wandering aimlessly about the grounds. After lunch they spent some time on the battlements, sprawled out and reading stacks of Sid's comics and magazines.

Alex was reading a vampire comic called *Tomb of Dracula* and despite the events of the past week his first feeling was guilty thrill. His father had always forbidden books on the supernatural—for the first time, Alex thought, he had a clue as to why. But still he couldn't help trying to compare the pale figures of the comic with those he had seen, even if he could not discuss them aloud.

"What was the first vampire book?" Alex asked.

Sid leaned back against the wall. "Modern vampire?"

"What does that mean?"

"I mean there were always stories about family ghosts that came back to haunt sons who'd embarrassed them," Sid said. "A modern vampire, that's the Dracula kind, a revived human who, you know, sucks blood and chases women."

"Okay."

"You have two important works in 1816—*Christabel* by Coleridge, but that's a poem and you want books," Sid went on, "so that brings us back to *The Vampyre* by John Polidori. Of course that one was really about Lord Byron."

"Lord Byron, the poet?" Paul asked. Alex remained quiet.

Sid nodded. "He was called Ruthven in the book,

but it's about how he would seduce and destroy every-one he met. It was clear to everyone that Polidori was writing about Byron. Byron was cruel, man. That girl Claire, Mary Shelley's half sister? She was obsessed with Byron and followed him everywhere, but when they had a child, Byron insisted on taking it and not letting Claire anywhere near it. Then he got tired of raising the baby and stuck her in a convent, where she died before she was six. He was a narcissist and a sadist. This guy was so bad, some people believe Polidori's vampire metaphor wasn't a metaphor at all."

Alex shook his head, impressed. "I'll take your word for it."

Sid stood up and looked over the battlements at the woods and the lake. "We have vampires *here.*"

"Come *on,*" Paul said, snorting. "There are no such things. Not in real life."

"What do you think happened to that woman in the square?" asked Sid insistently. "Just don't go in those woods at night, is all I'm saying."

Paul started snickering and Alex tried to join him. After a moment Paul said, "Do you ever look anything but sad?"

Alex smiled awkwardly. "Is that how I look?"

Paul rested his great forearms on his knees and said,

"When I got here—this is three years ago—I spent all my time thinking about Ealing. That was my neighborhood. I thought about it all the time. The parks where I rode my bike, my friends. It got where if I *wasn't* thinking about it I felt guilty for *not* thinking about it."

Sid nodded to Alex, indicating this was true.

Paul said, "So Count Dracula here started bugging me about London. Had I been to where they filmed those Hummer movies."

"Hammer," said Sid. "That's a vampire series."

"Hammer movies. Whatever. And there's classes, and there's answering all these bloody questions. And sooner or later, I realized that my life was here, at least for now."

"Your life was talking about your home instead of thinking about it?"

"My life was whatever was going on," Paul said. "What do you miss?"

"I don't know," said Alex, trying to think. "We watch a lot of old movies, that's my mom's thing. And I miss skiing with my sister." That wasn't quite accurate, unless one understood skiing to mean *rescue* skiing. His little sister Ronnie, although twelve, was already an enthusiastic search-and-rescue aficionado, and when they had lived in Wyoming she and Alex had both thrown themselves into the training they were lucky enough to receive. Ronnie was the most daring of his four siblings.

"So I have news for you, mate," Paul said. "You can keep that. But everybody back home would probably want you to make the best of your life here."

They cracked into the shojo that Sid had borrowed from Minhi.

When Alex looked at the first shojo, emblazoned with a great, black-winged angel holding a guitar, he saw her name scrawled on the back cover. "Minhi with an h," he said. He opened up the book and a slip of paper fell out, jagged and torn from Minhi's pink notebook. He picked it up. After reading it for a second, Alex asked, "Did you guys see this?"

Paul and Sid shook their heads. "What?" Paul asked.

Below the phone number and email address, the note said: FALL RECITAL AND MIXER. SATURDAY AT 8. LALAURIE SCHOOL.

"It's an invitation," Alex said, as he stood up. For a moment he leaned on the battlements, watching the lake, feeling a bit like a knight.

CHAPTER 10

At seven o'clock the boys gathered at the front gate on their bikes. They figured it would take forty-five minutes to make it around the lower horn of the lake to LaLaurie.

"You look quite posh," Paul said to Alex, who was wearing a school jacket he had borrowed from Sid—he hadn't received his own yet—and a pair of dress pants he had managed to lug back with a bag full of his other clothes from his old room.

Sid's jacket was a little small at the shoulders for Alex, but Paul's only extra had surrounded Alex like a shroud when he put it on, so he had decided to go with too tight.

They benefited from another thing that Paul explained. On Saturday, the ten o'clock curfew check was notoriously lax for the simple reason that the older boys tasked with enforcing it tended to be out themselves.

Around the weaving road they pedaled, moving at a steady clip as the sun went down, talking all the way. Paul and Sid filled Alex in on classes, teachers, school traditions. Everyone agreed that the librarian was hot but could probably rip you in half, and that Sangster was easily the most demanding teacher they had. Sid said that Mr. Otranto was known to have powers beyond those of mortal men when it came to anything he needed for the school or its students; he had once procured Russian visitor visas for the Glenarvon mathlete team in less than forty-eight hours. The guy was connected, but had no social life—or none anyone had observed. This was no accident: Teachers and staff all lived in a garden-style apartment complex on the far side of the campus, and students were not welcome to roam there. Alex took all of this in, deliriously happy to be rid of the colossal strangeness of the past several days.

Finally, they reached a well-manicured drive under an archway that read LALAURIE SCHOOL. The boys fell silent as they passed by brilliant topiaries and into an enormous parking area. They locked their bikes at a rack along a berm near the entrance. The lot was crowded with racing-green Jaguars and gray Rolls-Royces, Mercedes upon Mercedes.

Visitors were milling about the lawn as Alex, Paul, and Sid approached the front entrance. They reached the top of the wide, rounded staircase and hung to the side for a moment. "Let me do the talking," Paul said under his breath.

"Guys," came a voice.

They turned to see Sangster jogging up the steps in a dinner jacket and black pants. He was carrying an old, leather-bound book tied with a silver ribbon and bow.

"Mr. Sangster!" Sid gasped.

Alex was already trying to figure out how he'd followed them, but he realized that especially where Sangster was concerned, there were a thousand easy ways. "This is a surprise," Alex said.

"Yeah, I wish I'd known you guys were coming!" Sangster smiled. It occurred to Alex that Sangster the teacher was a different person from Sangster the . . . *whatever that other Sangster was.* The differences were subtle but there. He wondered if Sangster even noticed himself. The teacher added, "So does *anyone* know you were coming?"

Paul looked at the others, and then tried, "What really do you mean by *know*?"

Sangster waved him off. "Stop while you're ahead."

"Are you here on . . . business?" Alex asked darkly.

"Not really. So do you have an invitation?" Sangster looked up at the front gate, where a woman in a silk blouse held a clipboard and was checking names.

"Alex, the note is in your pack, mate—"

"*Kind* of. Actually," Alex said, "we were sort of winging it."

Sangster nodded. "All right then."

As they climbed the front steps, Alex quietly asked Sangster, "Did you really not know we'd be here?"

Sangster gave him a look that suggested Alex must think he had just fallen off a turnip truck. Then he pulled away and went up to the woman at the door. As Sangster approached, she showed a moment of confusion and then lit up with surprise. They hugged briefly and then Sangster indicated the book he'd brought. She registered more surprise, and then genuine appreciation.

Alex followed this few seconds of pantomime—they had met but didn't seem to know each other that well.

Now Sangster gestured back at the boys, squirming in their dress shoes, and Alex did make out the words, "Little fans."

Alex watched the woman wave her head from side to side, *Oh, all right.* She touched Sangster on the elbow.

And they were in.

The performance hall of LaLaurie School was off to the right. All in all it looked much like Glenarvon except with more flowers. The entryway to the performance hall spilled into a foyer where several of the students were rushing back and forth. There was excitement everywhere, and Alex felt a strange jealousy as he saw girls in uniforms introducing friends to friends and friends to parents and parents to teachers.

"I feel like an intruder," said Alex to Paul, who was reading a program. Sid was turning pale.

Suddenly a figure was waving from near the entrance of the auditorium. It was Minhi. She gestured with long, skinny arms for them all to come, and Sangster led them through the throngs, smiling faintly to Alex as they went.

"Look at you gentlemen with the jackets," she was saying.

"Yeah, I had to borrow mine, which is why it's so small," Alex volunteered idiotically. He sighed inwardly. *Moving along.* "You know Paul and Sid. This is our lit instructor, Mr. Sangster." Minhi made a slight curtsy.

"What are you performing?" Sangster asked.

"It says here . . ." Paul held up a program he'd been handed. "Well, I see 'ballet' and 'poetry' and 'singing,' and then there's you."

"Then there's me," she said, smiling wryly.

"You're not reading poetry, are you?" Alex asked.

"I'm not sure I'd invite you here for that," she said with a smile. She looked at her watch and said, "There are some seats down right. See you after the show."

Sangster, Alex, Paul, and Sid filed into the auditorium, found some seats, and settled in for a nightmare of several ballet pieces, three different solo vocal renditions of "Ave Maria," and lots . . . and lots . . . of poetry.

And then came Minhi.

She bounded upon the stage in a black tunic, black leggings, and bare feet, and began to demonstrate her own art. She moved fluidly, muscles tight, sliding through a routine that looked like a performance of karate but brought all its force driven inward, intense and contained. Minhi drew imaginary bows, brought her fists in and out with a power that seemed to bend on itself. Above all it was slow, so slow that her muscles seemed ready to spring and pop, always controlled, every punch hypnotically glacial in its movement.

"Kung fu?" whispered Alex.

"*Hung Gar*," whispered Sangster back. "Don't be fooled by the speed. She could knock your head off."

There were other performances, but Alex would recall none of them.

After the recital, Paul, Sid, Minhi, Alex, and Sangster abandoned the crowds and headed out a pair of French doors onto the enormous lawn, which ended at the lake. The sun had mostly set, but lanterns were lit around the perimeter of the lawn, which itself was studded with classical statues.

Alex competed with Paul and Sid in sheer enthusiasm. "That was—that was fantastic."

"You were like an action hero," said Sid.

"Again!" Alex said. "That's like the second time you've been an action hero. Hey, *he* said you could take someone's head off." Alex thumbed back at Sangster. Sangster raised an eyebrow, his hands in his pockets as he walked.

Minhi was leading them down to a floating pier at the edge of the water, smiling as she went. This had been her idea, to get away from all the families and alumni.

"Why isn't your family here?" Paul asked Minhi.

"It's a long way," Minhi said. "Still, I'll see them at the winter break."

Alex dropped back next to Sangster and changed his tone as his thoughts returned to the hunt for the Scholomance. He asked quietly, "How are your friends?"

"They're impatient," Sangster said, watching the lake. "How does an entire fortress hide in plain sight?"

"Were you going to find out last night?"

Sangster glanced at Alex. "Maybe. Never can tell. But we went one way and the caravan went the other. We missed the entrance this time."

"Could they be underground?"

"We've scanned," said Sangster. "All around the lake."

"What about"—Alex searched for the words—"extra-dimensional pockets?"

Sangster smiled. "You've seen too many movies."

As they reached the shore and the start of the narrow pier that led to the larger floating platform, which had railings and iron loops into which to place fishing poles, Alex heard someone call, "Mr. Sangster!" They all looked back.

Alex asked Minhi, "Who's that?"

"The assistant headmistress, Mrs. Daughtry," Minhi replied.

The woman was moving rapidly across the lawn toward them, but she was smiling. Sangster gave a small wave. "*Mrs.* Daughtry?"

The woman laughed. "It's not; it's Ms.," she corrected. She was holding the book Sangster had brought her and she gestured with it. "I remembered you from the Coleridge panel at the Brussels conference, but I was shocked you'd remember—"

"That you were looking for a second edition Blake?" Sangster finished her sentence. "Ah, I ran across it. Will you join us?"

Ms. Daughtry took Sangster's offered hand as they stepped over the pier onto the platform. "Why not?" she said. "Put yourself in my position. I've got four male visitors and one of my prize students."

"Well, she is a kung fu masstah," said Paul. Minhi punched him lightly on the arm.

Sangster turned to Alex, Sid, and Paul. "Ms. Daughtry is the assistant headmistress here at LaLaurie, but she's also a Victorian scholar. I read a paper of hers that made me change how I taught half my class." He leaned back on the railing and added, "Go ahead, admit it, the party was killing you."

Ms. Daughtry laughed. "So have you been to LaLaurie before?"

Sangster shook his head.

Sid was peppering Minhi with questions about her

art. "Do you have any weapons? You know, like silver sai?"

"That's really a different kind of kung fu," she said.

"Can you show us some more?" asked Paul.

Alex found himself feeling uneasy for no reason he could put his finger on. He watched Minhi begin demonstrating the bow stance, knees bent and center of gravity low as she drew back, when a shock of static and vibration shook his brain. The temperature dropped— *ten degrees? Twenty?* Minhi, still drawing her imaginary bow, turned with everyone else toward the water.

At first it appeared that a strange wave was whipping across the lake, water lifting and separating like the wake of a speedboat, except for two things—there was no boat, and the water froze.

Static exploding in his mind, Alex watched the expanse of ice stretch across the lake, all the way into the dark distance, shooting directly toward them.

Alex started gesturing at the school. "Come on," he said firmly, looking at his friends. *Get off the pier. Get inside.*

"What?" Minhi asked, bewildered. They were all looking at the ice.

"Trust me!"

Alex peered over his shoulder as they reached the

shore, and he could make out shapes on what now appeared to be a jagged frozen bridge. There were figures running through the fog that lay low across the water and the ice.

Alex looked back at Sangster. "It's him."

Sangster shouted, "Everyone, inside!"

As one, they began running. Alex was passing an enormous statue, some goddess in a chariot surrounded by birds, when the static mixed with a new sound that was both in his brain and out of it. The intruders—attackers—were chanting. He turned back for a second, pausing, unable to do anything but listen.

And suddenly they were there, hitting the shore. A figure gliding in off the water seemed to be gathering mist around him. As he approached, the air around the goddess statue froze, covering the marble chariot in ice. The tall man was coming fast. Farther up the lawn and on the porch of the school, the crowd was scrambling for cover, diving into the building. Only Alex and those who had been on the pier were still on the grass. Alex broke and ran for the entrance, catching up with Minhi and Ms. Daughtry, Paul and Sid. He looked back to see Icemaker punch right through the frozen statue, sending shards of marble everywhere.

Nearby, Sangster reached into his dinner jacket,

grabbing a handset and bringing it to his ear. "Farmhouse, this is Sangster at LaLaurie School—we are under attack by the Quarry."

After a second a voice shot back, "Describe force."

"It's dark; I see at least twenty, plus the big one," Sangster said, drawing his handgun and trying to find a target. Alex, the boys, Minhi, and Ms. Daughtry made it up onto the porch.

Alex yanked at the French doors. Paul and Sid banged on the glass panels. Through the glass Alex could see the students and teachers staring in disbelief.

"Let us in!" Minhi called. "Let us in!" No one inside would move.

Alex grabbed a wicker chair and brought it forward, beating upon the rear entrance. Useless. He looked around. He would need something better. He scanned the porch, finding a heavy ceramic flower pot, roughly the size of a person's head. He grasped it by the wire hangers and swung it against the French doors.

The glass crunched and the crowd stepped back, still frozen in panic, whatever sense of guilt they possessed leaving them as unwilling to hinder him as they were to help.

Alex said, "Okay," and reached through the broken glass to turn the deadbolt, not caring about being cut.

He got the door open. To his right something grabbed Paul. Alex lunged for him but the vampire was too fast, dragging Paul toward the shore by the ankles. Sid and Minhi were watching in horror; on the lawn, Sangster was already pursuing the vampire that had grabbed Paul. Then another vampire struck Sangster hard from the side, sending him sprawling.

Slow motion: Sangster grunting as he hit the ground. Alex shouting, "Get inside" to Sid and Minhi, leaping off the porch in pursuit of Paul. The vampire that had tackled Sangster was dashing forward, zipping from the lawn to the porch, grabbing Minhi by the ankle.

"No!" Alex yelled, running flat out. But he was losing ground already. Behind him Sangster struggled to rise, beset by yet another attacking vampire in red. Alex sprinted as hard as he could. *This doesn't happen. Minhi and Paul are being carried away.*

The tall vampire, the one floating over the shore while his minions did their work, whipped his head around to Alex, settling a glowing pair of eyes upon him. *Icemaker.* The clan lord sent a boulder-size chunk of ice directly toward Alex, who threw himself to the side just in time.

Icemaker had flowing black locks that curled over his shoulders, and Alex realized his great height owed to legs that were distended unnaturally, iced over at the calves, giving him the appearance of a hoofed demon. He wore an armored doublet of red, and his eyes blazed with cold. Alex caught a glimpse of Paul and Minhi being dragged out onto the iced-over lake. He picked himself up, thinking only of getting past this vampire, of getting to his friends. He began to move.

There was a *fwooshing* sound as Sangster destroyed the vampire he was fighting. A hail of bullets rained past Alex as Sangster came running, firing at Icemaker. The bullets blew chunks of ice off the armor on the vampire's shoulders and chest. "Alex, get back!" Sangster shouted. Icemaker swept toward Alex, freezing and shattering the blades of grass as he went. The vampire ignored Sangster's bullets and stopped mere feet from Alex, who likewise found himself halting, unable to look away.

"Joining the family business, are we?" Icemaker snarled. His voice sounded brittle, low, and ragged. "Do you seriously think you pose any threat to me at all?"

The vampire lifted off the ground and began to swoop backward toward the water as the air swirled and congealed up and down the beach. Alex was staring at a wall of ice.

They were gone.

Alex fell to his knees.

Sangster reached Alex's side. "Minhi and Paul?"

"Yes," Alex groaned. "What about Sid?"

"He's safe. He's inside." Sangster stepped back, surveying the wall of ice. "Look!"

Alex rose and staggered back to read the words carved into the icy wall.

WELCOME TO THE COLD.

CHAPTER 11

Minhi lost her balance the moment she felt her ankle yanked out from under her and she fell back, catching the porch with her shoulders. She tried to use her moves, twisting and kicking at the woman who was dragging her off. She saw Paul's head bounce on the grass and then on *ice* as he was dragged beside her.

They were being towed onto the lake itself, moving fast. The woman who had Minhi slacked her grip a bit as she began to "skate" with her feet across the ice. Minhi took the advantage to twist, hard, and suddenly she was free.

Minhi sprawled out, spinning on what she now saw was actually an ice road that stretched across the lapping waves of Lake Geneva. She found her footing, glancing back at the shore. She slipped as she started to run, then gingerly looked for cracks and crevices in the ice, picking up the pace.

Suddenly the attacker came at her again. The villain laughed, tufts of dark hair sticking out from the red wrap around her head. Her teeth showed, long and glistening. *Vampires?* Shocked, Minhi missed her opportunity to dodge the woman.

This time the creature wrapped one arm around Minhi's torso, grabbing her tight. Minhi was no match for her.

"What are you—where are we going?" Minhi begged.

"We're going home," hissed the vampire.

After a few minutes of seeming to fly over the frozen road, a voice filled the air, cold as ice. *"Though I be ashes, a far hour shall wreak the deep prophetic fullness of this verse."*

Minhi could see a man, floating on the air, surrounded by icy wind, the moon behind him. They were nearing another shore. She saw a great house there, a ghostly manor surrounded by trees, and at the shoreline, the sculpture of an angel, its arms held wide.

They were headed for the sculpture. Now just at the

edge of the shore the ice disappeared, and there were waves churning.

The man was enjoying himself. *"And pile on human heads the mountain of my curse!"*

They rapidly approached the sculpture and then plunged down through the churning water. Minhi's vision was swimming as the water *disappeared* and they entered a dry tunnel. Down into the tunnel, down over dank and shimmering stone, down past support beams of skull and bone, down past torches the vampires ran, their feet light, running like wolves.

And then they arrived, far below, coming to a stop in what Minhi could only call a courtyard, vast and groomed with spiny grass as white as bone.

The vampire holding Minhi threw her to the ground and she rolled to a stop, coming to her knees. She was shaking in terror.

Paul was nearby. In his eyes Minhi could see the same fear that she felt. She stood, dizzy, and looked up to see an enormous castle, all under the lake—under the very lake! Up to the dark sky of rock the walls reached, rock and mud reinforced with latticeworks of more bone.

The captors stood around them, waiting. Minhi became aware of more figures, standing on the battlements of the castle and lining the edges of the courtyard. Many of them, like Minhi's attackers, wore red, but the vast majority wore white tunics and hoods. Beneath those hoods, white, white skin glowed in the darkness. And their eyes reflected the light of the torches, so that as Minhi looked out, she saw hundreds upon hundreds of pairs of glowing eyes.

"What is this?" Minhi whispered.

"This," the voice boomed from behind her. She turned slowly, petrified to look. A great vampire with long hair and wearing red armor was drifting to the ground on an icy wind. "This . . . is the Scholomance!"

CHAPTER 12

Alex and Sid hurtled down the road in the back of a Glenarvon Academy van with Sangster at the wheel. Periodically the teacher looked at both of them through the rearview mirror as trees zipped by.

"I told you!" Sid said desperately. He jumped up, shaking Alex. "I told you vampires were real! Those were—"

"Sid," Sangster called, "I need you to sit down."

"All right, what was that?" Sid demanded. "Who *were* those people?"

"I don't know," Sangster called back, locking eyes with Alex through the mirror for a second. "I don't know. We need to get back to the school. They need to know that there's been a kidnapping and you guys need to be back in your rooms."

"They came from the *lake*," said Sid, nearly delirious. "They were *vampires*."

"*Terrorists*," Sangster said evenly. "I think they were terrorists. My concern is getting you guys to safety."

Alex said nothing. He watched the horizon in front of the van, the dark road lit up by high beams, trees flying past on either side.

Within minutes they ripped off the road to the front gate and Sangster was hustling them out.

Mrs. Hostache was waiting in a housecoat by the door. "I got your call," she said. "What do we know about Paul?"

"All I know is what I told you," Sangster said, guiding Alex and Sid inside. "I was watching all three. The terrorists came up off the water. They did a lot of distracting stuff and grabbed two people—one was Paul." Alex noted that Sangster was using the word *terrorist* every chance he got, and he understood why: Sangster was making sure the word would be seeded into the narrative and get repeated often.

She shook her head gravely. "Come on, come in," she said.

"Did you speak with the police?" Sangster asked.

"*Oui*," Mrs. Hostache said, nodding. "They are at

LaLaurie. They should have questions for us in the morning." Now she turned to Alex and Sid and knelt slightly, as though they were eight. "How are you two?"

Alex opened his hands, as if to say, "I have no idea." Sid had no response.

"To bed with you," Mrs. Hostache said. "We'll talk in the morning."

Sangster was standing next to the stairs as Alex and Sid went up, and he stopped them, patting both their shoulders firmly. As he did so, Alex felt Sangster slip a note under the collar of his jacket.

After he and Sid numbly went to bed, unable to form words, Alex unfolded the note. It said: *Midnight*.

"What is *that*?"

When Alex snuck out an hour and a half later, Sangster was waiting just outside the school gate. Alex found the teacher seated on his motorcycle. Next to him, lit by moonlight dappling through the trees, was a new gunmetal gray—

"Kawasaki Ninja," said the teacher. "It's not as big as most of the bikes we use, but it's more powerful than most of your smaller motorcycles out there."

Alex approached the bike, moving slowly around it. On the gray right flank he saw the emblem of the

Polidorium, which he had seen before on the vans and other vehicles. There was that motto in Latin, *Talia sunt*. "What do these words mean, anyway? '*Talia sunt*.'"

"It means 'there are such things.'" Sangster tossed Alex a pair of night-vision GPS goggles. "Come on. Let's go figure out how to get Paul and Minhi back."

Alex was glad he was wearing his contacts, because he doubted he could wear the goggles over his glasses. They were tighter than the ones he had worn last night—*Was it only last night?* Next he donned the gray helmet he found resting on the seat of the bike.

Once the helmet was on, Alex could hear Sangster in his ear through the onboard speaker. "Copy?"

"I thought you didn't want me in on this stuff?"

"Icemaker spoke to you, Alex," said Sangster, as he started his own bike and began to roll. "You're in it. Plus . . . I think I could use your ability to sense them."

They eased out onto a two-lane highway that ran along the lake and began to lay down tracks, heading south.

They traveled about ten kilometers in silence with nary a car in sight, the world dark but for the occasional zip of a street lamp, and then flew off the road down the dirt track that led to the farmhouse.

Past the ornamental tin wall of the farmhouse and down into the earth once more. Within minutes they were in Director Carerras's conference room.

"All right," Sangster said, bringing up a map of Lake Geneva. "What is he up to?"

"First things first," Carerras barked. "I agreed to let you bring the Van Helsing boy here, but you had better come up with a reason." Armstrong, who sat to the director's right, leaned back, raising her eyebrow in agreement.

Alex preempted Sangster. "I got face-to-face with Icemaker," he said. "He spoke to me."

Carerras leaned forward. "What did he say?"

"He asked if I was joining the family business," Alex said. "And he suggested that I wasn't going to be any good at it."

"They were watching him at Glenarvon," Sangster ticked off. "And they attacked us in full view of everyone tonight. They know who he is, and they *know he's here.* Icemaker wants that family. It was Charles's father who stopped him at the Louvre Museum, remember? And Charles destroyed nearly five hundred of Icemaker's disciples in Cuba. I'm willing to bet they got wind of Alex the first time he swept his passport at Geneva airport."

"Do you think he kidnapped Minhi and Paul because

they were with me?" Alex asked in horror. They had been dragged away before his eyes.

Sangster sighed. "I—Alex, that's not how it looked. I think taunting you was just a bonus. But this was about getting attention. He wanted us to see him. This was a big move."

"We'll have to pay a lot of people to smooth this over in the press," Carerras grumbled.

Seriously, you do that?

"So Icemaker now has hostages," Sangster continued. "Why? What do we know about him—why would he come back here, and what is he going to do here that he would need hostages?"

Sangster brought up Icemaker's dossier on the screen, and Alex saw there a stippled drawing of Icemaker where a photograph would normally be, followed by dates and other information. It looked like one of Sid's characters.

"The last time he was here was when he *first* began to succumb to vampirism, that Haunted Summer when Polidori was still his friend," Sangster said. "When they were staying at the Villa Diodati."

Sangster scrolled down the dossier. Remembering, Alex said, "You said something about Icemaker destroying a ship."

"Yeah." Sangster reached the most recent activity in

the dossier. "He plundered and sank a Polidorium cargo vessel called the *Wayfarer*, and immediately started heading this way."

"And you have no idea what he *got* off that ship?"

"We have a manifest of a thousand items," Sangster responded. "Books, scrolls, statues, gauntlets. It's all lost. Anything could be useful to him, but nothing we can narrow down."

"We can assume," interjected Armstrong, "that someone leaked him the manifest, which would suggest he knew what he was looking for."

"So," said Alex, "he stole something or learned something on the ship. He comes here to the . . ."

"Scholomance," said Carerras.

" . . . The Scholomance. And now he's kidnapped two of my friends. I'll tell you what I think it means."

"What's that?"

Alex wrung his hands. "It means what in the name of all that is holy are you people wasting time for? Go get them!"

"We have to find it first," said Sangster. "And we're trying."

"You may have a new lead," interjected Carerras, who appeared completely unfazed by Alex's emotion. "Armstrong?"

Armstrong tapped a key in front of her and a new image came up on the screen—the lake, overlaid by wavy, undulating lines labeled WIND PATTERN.

"When Icemaker struck we turned one of the satellites on the lake. We lost track of him in a burst of cold air and clouds, but we noted key disruptions in the normal wind pattern here," she said, indicating a point along the shore.

"What's that?" Alex asked.

"That," said Sangster, leaning forward, "would be the Villa Diodati, where it all began."

CHAPTER 13

"Minhi!"

Minhi's eyes flickered open and she felt her stomach heave; the room was moving. She was resting on a floor, an iron floor, and there were bars against her shoulders. She realized she was in a *cage*. She rose, putting her hands on the bars, looked out, and screamed. The room wasn't moving; she was swinging.

Her scream echoed through the vast, torchlit hall where hundreds of vampires were gathered. Only a few bothered to look up. "Minhi!" came the voice again. It was Paul, in the next cage over. They were suspended some twenty feet off the ground.

Below them, the tall head vampire was pacing on a

raised stage between the cages and the gathered audience.

"What's going on?" she said to Paul.

"I have no idea," Paul said, rubbing the back of his head. "I think they knocked us out. Are you all right?"

"I'm okay," she said, "but this can't be happening." Looking out across the hall, she saw banners that flowed from ceiling to floor, bearing a crest and the word *Scholomance*. Between a couple of the banners was a huge clock, the face of which seemed to be made of bone. It was a few minutes to midnight.

"No, now listen," Paul said. "It is happening. It is. But we're alive. All right? That's a good sign."

"What makes you think it's a good sign?"

"Because," Paul said, "if they wanted to kill us they would have done it already. So probably this is about money."

"Money?" Minhi demanded. "They're monsters."

"Even monsters need money," Paul observed.

They sat quietly for a few moments, cross-legged in their own cages. After a while Paul folded his arms and sighed. "I must tell you: This was not my plan for a first date."

"There was a plan?"

The Icemaker began to speak.

"Vampires!" The ice-hoofed vampire strode onto the stage, his lip curled in a sneer. "Since time immemorial, we have been the uncrowned masters of the earth. Is it not so?" He looked around. Near the stage, the leading vampires from the school nodded, rapt in attention.

Minhi listened in silence, taking in every word. This was insane. This was a dream. A floating vampire with long hair and glowing eyes, around whom the air froze as he moved, was speaking to a roomful of more vampires who worshipped him. The world had gone mad.

Minhi saw the vampire's white eyes fall on her and Paul. There was cold even in his gaze. "Look there. Cattle. As insignificant as the humans we bring in from the forgotten corners of the cities on which to feed. But these cattle are special. They will be our sacrifice."

Icemaker returned his eyes to the crowd. "I cannot lead the Scholomance into greatness alone. There is one whose deviancy and deviousness dwarfed my own, and who I must have as my queen. But we will need to make a great sacrifice to raise her—for she was a human, unjustly punished in life, now lost to death.

"There is a demon that can help us raise my new queen," Icemaker said, "but for hundreds of years I have sought the secret of this demon without success. Until this."

Minhi watched as Icemaker produced a leather scroll wrapped around an iron scepter. The tip of the scepter was a foxlike head, with human eyes and long, pointed ears.

"Without this scroll we did not know the words or the sacrifice that would move the demon," Icemaker continued. "For years it was hidden from us by a small man, a pitiful mortal. But now we are ready. To spill the blood we must spill, to say the words we must say, and afterward, to receive the new power that will change this world forever." He put the scroll down.

"The demon's name is *Nemesis*," said the vampire, "and the queen she will raise is . . . Claire."

CHAPTER 14

Even with the aid of the in-helmet GPS, it took another quarter hour for Alex and Sangster to reach the Villa Diodati, which stood on the south-southwest shore of the lake. It was a vast, stucco-covered manor, perfectly square, threatened on all sides by trees that seemed to Alex to be attempting to pull the place into the ground. Alex followed Sangster to the sloping bank on the eastern side, where the balustrades of the balcony, like large teeth, made the house look thirsty.

They stopped their bikes in the vineyards before the house and stood in silence for a moment, surrounded by the sounds of the lapping waves of the lake and the chirps of frogs and night birds.

"Why are we here?" Alex asked. A dull, muted static was beginning to throb in his head, though, and he thought he knew the answer.

Sangster took off his helmet, laid it on his handlebars, and brought a smaller headset out of his shirt pocket and up to his ear. Then he pulled a leather pack out of the saddlebags and threw it over his shoulder. "In truth," he said, "there is no reason the Scholomance should be at Lake Geneva at all. Bram Stoker said it was in Eastern Europe and we killed decades looking there."

Alex shook his head slowly in wonder. "How can you treat a novel as though it were a history book?"

Sangster said, "We weren't making plans based on *The Shining*, Alex. Remember: We know that the events of Stoker's *Dracula* actually happened, with a few embellishments. Our organization has a memory that goes back to Van Helsing before Bram Stoker even wrote his book. Besides, Stoker admitted all this while he was still alive."

"Really? When?"

"In his introduction to the 1901 Icelandic edition," Sangster said. "Will there be anything else?"

"Just that I'd love to see you go toe to toe with Sid." Alex looked around. "It's strange. I'm feeling something like that thing, that static I feel when they're near," he said. "But it's distant."

Sangster nodded. "This confirms my suspicions. There is evil in this place."

"So why? Why Lake Geneva?"

Sangster rolled his neck, considering. "The lake has always attracted people interested in vampires and the supernatural. Besides the Diodati party, Yeats was here; Milton was here; Coleridge was here. The villa itself is very impressive; you'll find art of all kinds, paintings of great literature, lots of myths. But so far, there is no entrance to the Scholomance to be found. And we have ways of finding secret entrances. You see this vineyard?" Sangster was walking toward the shore, then looked back at the trees. "A year ago we tried looking in and all around it, hoping something would open up."

"Open up? You mean like, 'Open Sesame,' and the ground rolls away?"

"The clan lords and others on their level are able to hide behind powerful energy fields. With the right tools we can drop these fields, but you have to find them. And all around here—the house itself, the vineyards, all around the statue—we tried. Nothing."

"But the entrance is here after all?"

"Well, we didn't look in the water," Sangster said. Now he spoke into his headset. "Armstrong, you on?"

"Copy."

"What are you seeing?"

"Wind twenty knots, southeast."

"Pockets?"

"Wind is bouncing off the house, bouncing off the trees—I have your position, there is nothing in front of you. Wait—"

"What?"

"There's a bounce of wind, a dip, about fifteen meters north of your position."

"All right, stand by." Sangster took a few long steps. He reached into his pack and produced a long mesh strap of glass balls about the size of his fist. They clinked as he strung them over his shoulder.

Sangster slipped one of the glass balls out of the strap and tossed it to Alex. Alex caught it, feeling its weight—the ball was about half again as heavy as a baseball. "What's this?"

"Holy water."

Sangster crouched, removing a leather roll from his pack, which he lay open to reveal more tools. He drew out what appeared to be a stake with an ornate handle and handed it to Alex. "Keep this with you. Remember—with a vampire you need to hit the heart to kill. Best shot is right between the ribs—here," and he tapped Alex to the left of his sternum. "Okay?"

Alex noticed a two-foot-long contraption of wood and metal. The device was fully enclosed in dark material, with a silver trigger and a large housing in the front that appeared to contain the works of the weapon. "That looks like a—crossbow."

"It's a Polibow," Sangster said, nodding. "It doesn't get damaged as easily as a crossbow, but it's as quiet. You have a cartridge that fits in the top, loaded with silver shafts threaded with wood. Twelve of them."

"Silver," Alex repeated. In old movies, silver was for werewolves and the Lone Ranger, who when you got down to it could probably hunt werewolves really well. "And are your bullets silver, too?"

"Silver and *wood*. Our bullets are pressed hawthorn wood with a silver jacket."

"Isn't all that a lot more expensive than lead?"

"Much, but lead doesn't kill vampires," Sangster said, stopping in his crouch. "Only wood and silver do. Silver is actually more an allergen; wood alone will kill. When it comes to wood, hawthorn is best."

"Why's that?"

Sangster tapped his own forehead. "The crown of thorns was made from it. Your stake is made of hawthorn. Holy stuff burns the bejesus out of them. But to kill, you gotta get 'em in the heart."

"Anything else?" Alex wanted to know. It would be useful to have information *before* he needed it for once.

Sangster thought through a list he seemed to keep in his head as he continued rummaging in his pack. "Direct sunlight will burn up the younger ones."

"But not the older ones?" Alex asked.

"On a cloudy day you might find them in the market," said Sangster. "Shopping for shoppers."

Sangster seemed to find what he was looking for—a folding device that looked like a pocketknife. He closed up and stuffed the roll in his pack, then drew from his own shoulder holster a pistol with a silencer on the end. He unfolded the pocketknife-like device and it came apart into two large pieces. One unfolded further into the shape of a rifle stock, which Sangster now snapped into the back of the pistol. The other device slotted into the top of the gun, and by the glint of glass on the end Alex could see it was a gun sight. Now Sangster brought the gun up to his shoulder.

"We're gonna do some skeet shooting. Gimme a good throw—put 'er right over there," he said, indicating the general direction of the water.

"Over the water?" Alex hefted the ball, gauging how he would throw it.

"Yep. Not too far, about twenty meters."

Alex drew back and threw, letting the ball arc high, then down about twenty meters out. Sangster moved smoothly, and there was a *shoomp* sound, followed by a tinkling as the ball exploded.

Sangster frowned. "No."

"Wind can do all kinds of crazy things," Armstrong said from the radio. "Try twenty yards farther up—that would be a beeline from the front entrance to the house."

"Good," Sangster agreed, nodding to Alex. They moved farther up. "Pull."

Alex grinned at the idea that he was lunging a clay pigeon and threw, watching the glass ball arc high and glimmering. Another explosion. Nothing.

Sangster stopped. For a moment he slouched, and Alex feared that they had reached the end of it. The lead would not pan out.

Feeling sour and defeated, Alex stuck his hands in his pockets and scanned back south along the beach.

The static was still there, like a distant hiss, a TV left on in a room far away. He looked down the beach, watching the slowly churning surf, the sand and grass. About thirty meters away stood a statue of an angel, its arms spread wide.

"Whoa," said Alex. When his eyes scanned across the

angel, the hiss seemed to spike, as if someone in that faraway room had turned up the volume.

Alex ran down the beach, listening. For a couple moments there was almost nothing there again. The whole static thing was such a strange phenomenon that he barely knew how to feel it. But he kept running toward the statue.

He looked back to see Sangster following and heard the teacher say, "What about fifty meters south?"

Alex stopped before the angel guarding the lake. An inscription on the base of the statue read, BEHOLD IT, HEAVEN! HAVE I NOT HAD TO WRESTLE WITH MY LOT? The static was whispering louder now, as Alex looked at the angel. Then he turned toward the water, and the static sang.

Sangster caught up, reading the inscription aloud. "*Behold it, Heaven*," he said. "These are Byron's verses. *Pull*."

Alex drew back once more and threw, high and out, and as the ball tumbled toward the moon-specked waves, it seemed to freeze in place. Sangster drew a bead as it fell, and time stretched out. Alex swore he could feel the bullet find its place. The ball exploded, glass tinkling in all directions over the lake, and the holy water inside sprayed out.

There was a pop, a sizzle on the waves, or rather over

them, a momentary shimmer that spread out in a web about four meters wide. Then all was normal.

"Again," Sangster said.

Another ball. Contact. The cloud of holy water burst over the waves, and now the air shrieked and spat with electric protest, and then it sizzled and churned away. Alex gasped at what remained.

There in the lake was a slope, dark walls shimmering in the gloom. Water lapped lightly over the lip of the entrance, held in place by some power Alex could only imagine.

Alex said urgently, "Can we—should we go in, can we go?"

Sangster nodded toward the entrance, and now the air began to shimmer again, closing up as before. After a moment the reflection of the moon lay across the water as if nothing had disturbed it.

"You won't get through now," Sangster said.

Alex turned back to look at the angel, and behind it, the Villa Diodati. Nearby he could hear Sangster speaking into his headset. "Polidorium, we have located the Scholomance."

CHAPTER 15

"Hey! Hey, Alex!"

Alex forced his eyes open. It was Sunday morning. It couldn't be more than two, three hours later. "Huh?"

"Come on, get up," came Sid's voice. "Let's get something to eat."

Alex rubbed his face. "I mean seriously, you have to be kidding."

As he sat up, Alex looked across the room to see Sid going through the motions of combing his hair at the mirror of the small bathroom. "How long have you been up?"

Sid looked at Alex through the mirror as he wet his comb. "Not long; I overslept, too," Sid replied.

"No news this morning?" Alex asked, trying to think of what would be the thing to say if he had no information at all.

"You mean about Paul?" Sid came out of the bathroom. "No. Nothing."

In one of the lounges Alex and Sid passed, a TV was again playing news, where the lead story was that LaLaurie School for Girls had been the site of a terrorist attack that culminated in the abduction of two students. In the background behind the reporter, Alex could see workmen struggling to remove chunks of ice on the lawn—chunks that, the reporter was saying, no one could explain.

Alex and Sid continued in silence to breakfast. The tension in the school was terrible, much worse than it had been on the day of the Secheron fight. The absence of Paul seemed to give off waves around his usual seat. They sat in silence for a while before Alex got up to go into the kitchen to get some more orange juice. "Hey, killer," Alex heard as he walked by the Merrills' table. Bill and Steven were smirking at him.

"What did you say?"

"I called you a killer," said Bill. "That's it, isn't it? I thought you were some kind of deviant at your old school, but now that you've gotten Paul killed, it seems to me you're probably one of those people who bad things just . . . happen around."

"You don't know what you're talking about," said Alex angrily. "No one even knows where Paul is."

"*Do* you make bad things happen around you?"

Alex felt his fist ball up, a rush of blood to his face, waves of adrenaline flooding up in his chest. He was seeing Paul dragged away by his ankle, Minhi and Paul screaming. He felt himself start to growl as he drew back his hand.

Sid clapped him on the shoulder, suddenly there. "Hey," Sid said. The smaller boy seemed at once pleading and demanding. "Not now. Come on."

"No, I think he had an answer for us," Steven said unexpectedly, stepping forward. "What was it, Van Helsing?"

Alex found himself chest to chest with Steven when Sangster's voice rang out, bringing them out of their faceoff. "Alex! Sid!" Sangster cried. "Come here."

The teacher was standing at the door of the refectory. With a final scowl at the Merrills, Alex strode over to Sangster, Sid following closely.

"How are you two holding up?" he asked. "Besides this insane need to keep fighting with the Merrills."

"I didn't . . . ," Alex began, but Sid cut him off.

"We're just waiting for more news," Sid said.

Sangster nodded, and glancing from Sid to Alex, said, "Look, I know this may be an awkward time, but can you two do some research for me? For class."

Alex looked at Sid.

"Sure," said Sid, "anything to take my mind off this."

"I want to know about Lord Byron and magic," Sangster said. "I'm going to the library to pull whatever I can. Would you mind helping?"

Sid and Alex nodded and they were off.

The three of them went to the library where Sangster had set up at a long table in the back. Sangster's chair had several yellow legal pads and a stack of books laid before it. Sangster pulled a legal pad toward him, scrawled a library code on a slip of paper, and handed it to Sid. "Sid, I missed this one, could you go find it?"

Sid nodded, taking off for the stacks.

"It's taking some doing." Sangster looked at Alex. "But I'm on the move tonight."

"What do you mean 'it's taking some doing'?" Alex asked. "We found the entrance."

"Oh, they're happy about the entrance," Sangster said. "What they're not happy about is spending men and material on chasing after two hostages. They're afraid if we do something big and bold, we might lose access to the Scholomance."

Alex was disgusted. "What are you saying, that they'd sacrifice my friends because saving them would be inconvenient?"

"Alex," Sangster said, scowling. "We're not a bunch of Republic serial villains. To answer your question, yes, they *would* sacrifice the innocent if it would save *more lives*. If accessing the Scholomance *later*, with a bigger plan, when we know more, will save more lives, then they won't move right now. But beyond that, doesn't this spell *trap* to you? Just two hostages, taken right in front of me, a known agent to them, and you, a guy who they're just waiting to see hit the stage?"

Alex had to blanch at the idea that the vampire world was buzzing about getting him "onstage," as though he were a new Jonas Brother. "But you are going," he said. It was not a question.

"Yeah, I'm going," Sangster said. "I argued for hours. I'm not giving up on a student. They'll allow a one-man insertion. One try. That's it."

"Let me ask you something," Alex said. "You really think they're still alive?"

"I think so," Sangster said.

"Why do you think so?" Alex asked. His fear about

Paul and Minhi had been haunting him.

"Because you don't take two hostages right in front of witnesses just to kill them immediately afterward." Sangster scrawled another number on a slip and handed it to Alex. "So . . . at worst, it's probably a trap. But Icemaker is still up to something, and I need to figure out what that is. Here—I need some stuff on the whole Icemaker circle, Mary Shelley, Polidori, everyone. Go find this."

Alex turned around, looking at the slip of paper. The book was *The Monsters*, call letters 823 HOO. Alex scanned the vast bookshelves as he walked past them until he found the row marked 810–830.

It took Alex no time to locate the book Sangster had sent for—it was a new book on the Romantics and clearly had just been acquired and library-bound. When Alex found it, he pulled it down, stuck it under his arm, and scanned nearby to see if anything else might prove useful. He liked to stumble across information this way—visually scanning nearby books beat out online key word searches any day. His search paid off: He found another volume—*Polidori and the Vampires*—that made the hair on the back of his neck stand up.

Then he heard a creak. A book fell from a top shelf.

Alex looked up and then straight ahead at the sound

of a sharp laugh. Through the stacks, for just a moment, he saw the face of Steven Merrill. And then something heavy struck him across the forehead. As it tumbled down—it appeared to be a copy of *Childe Harold*—Alex was stunned. He tried to stand up straight, grab the bookshelf, but it was falling, books pouring in a wave off the shelf. Alex started to stumble and trip toward the aisle.

Slow motion now, the fourteen-foot-tall shelf began to crash down against the next one, domino reaching for domino, with Alex underneath. Suddenly, he felt something grab him across the waist and push him hard. Alex tumbled out into the aisle and fell spread-eagle on the floor. Safe.

The library shook and thundered, shelving units slamming down, heavy wooden sounds followed by thousands upon thousands of smaller falling-books sounds.

And then all was quiet. Alex staggered to his feet, looking back for who had hit him. There was Sangster, halfway buried under the shelves, trying to pry himself free.

Sangster cursed, then looked at Alex. "Help me with this," he rasped.

Now Sid came running up, followed by more students and the librarian. They all worked to lift the shelf off

Sangster's legs until finally there was enough give that the librarian, who was a strapping Viking of a woman, was able to grab Sangster by his shoulders and help him wriggle free.

Everyone let the shelves settle back. "Don't get up." The librarian held out her hand. "Can you feel your legs?"

Sangster was touching them. "Yes, yes, but . . ." He indicated his right leg, gritting his teeth. "I think this one is broken."

"You!" the librarian looked at Alex. "Go to the front and call an ambulance."

Alex was scanning the library for the Merrills, but they were nowhere in sight. As he ran to the front for the phone, he was cursing them, plotting indescribable revenge. If Sangster was hurt—if Sangster couldn't do the mission tonight, and the Polidorium was unwilling to do it without Sangster—where did that leave Paul and Minhi's chances for survival?

CHAPTER 16

"It's just a sprain." Sangster was waving off the protestations of Mrs. Hostache, who was adjusting a pillow that a nurse had put behind Sangster's head when they had led him into the emergency room. Sangster was in a curtained area of the ER in Secheron's clinic. Alex and Sid had ridden along on the condition that they remain silent and not interfere.

The doctor had already bound up Sangster's leg in a plastic-and-foam cast that prevented him from bending it. He would wear it, the doctor had said, for nearly a month. That would be weeks in a wheelchair or on crutches. Now they were just waiting for his wheels.

"Do you ever manage to go anywhere without

triggering some catastrophe?" asked Mrs. Hostache, staring at Alex. He could read what she was thinking—she was running through possibilities, angles: What would cause an enormous bookshelf to topple; whether such an occurrence could be caused by climbing or other roughhousing; or whether it intimated something definitely darker. Whether Alex had made it happen. Whether she trusted Alex or not. Especially given his record.

Alex cleared his throat. "If Mr. Sangster hadn't jumped and pushed me when he did, I—those things are heavy, is all I'm saying."

"How did this happen?" she finally asked, straining for a neutral tone.

He could tell the truth—he had seen the Merrills, and naturally they hated him and were inclined to try something nasty. But then had he seen them pushing, climbing, anything? Was it enough to stick? Finally he said, "I don't know."

"Were you climbing on the shelves?" Mrs. Hostache asked, pushing up her glasses.

I'm not four, Alex wanted to say, but instead he just shook his head honestly. "No, absolutely not."

"He wasn't climbing," said Sangster, rolling his eyes. "I thought I might have heard some kids roughhousing, but by the time I got there, the shelves were falling."

"Here we are." A nurse, a twenty-two-year-old ponytailed guy, arrived with a wheelchair for Sangster. "Your ride, m'sier."

"I can take the crutches," Sangster said, pointing to the ones by the bed.

"Hospital policy, m'sier, is to wheel you out. After that, eh, you can *run* as far as we are concerned." The nurse laughed.

Sangster shrugged. "Alex, carry those crutches to the front entrance, would you?"

Alex carried the crutches and the entourage followed Sangster out. When they hit the front door, Sid got into the back of the van as Mrs. Hostache climbed in and started it up.

As Alex helped Sangster into the van, he spoke low. "What about the raid?"

"The official position is wait and see; the raid is my idea." Sangster shook his head in disgust. "I'll be healed up soon."

The engine was running, and now Alex slowed to a crawl in helping Sangster out of the chair and onto the crutches. "How long will that take? The doctor said weeks."

"It's not ideal." Sangster sighed. "But trust me; it won't be that bad."

"That's *insane*," Alex hissed.

"*Shh,*" Sangster said. "Calm down."

"Have you called in yet?"

"No," said Sangster.

"So then is the Polidorium still thinking that you're going tonight?"

"They've given me reluctant permission and there's a go package waiting for me under the angel statue," Sangster said. "So it gets stalled."

Paul and Minhi may not have that kind of time, Alex thought to himself.

At ten o'clock, Alex rose and found Sid staring at him from his bunk. He was lying still on his side, watching silently. Alex remained wordless as he pulled on a pair of jeans and a hooded sweatshirt. It wasn't until he sat on the chair at the writing desk that Sid spoke.

"Where are you going?"

"Oh," Alex said, pulling on a pair of sneakers. "I forgot the—I left a—"

"Are you hunting them?"

Alex looked up. He had no idea how to answer, and he played out several versions in his head. Then he said truthfully: "I'm going to the Villa Diodati."

"That would be a secret, wouldn't it?" Sid asked.

Alex finished lacing his shoes. "Yeah."

"Then I was asleep." Sid turned over to face the wall.

Alex nodded, rising. "I need to borrow your bike again."

"Just get them *back*."

Alex rode Sid's bike a quarter mile down the road before ditching it behind a small group of pine trees, where he and Sangster had hidden the Kawasaki Ninja in the early hours of the morning on the way back from the shore. He pulled several branches and a tarp off the motorcycle. It took him another twenty minutes to reach the vineyards of the Villa Diodati.

CHAPTER 17

Static throbbed and hissed in the back of Alex's head as he crept along the beach near the Villa Diodati. The angel statue cast its gaze on the water, its wings unfurled, its arms wide and beckoning. Alex bent down, sweeping sand aside next to the marble base. After a moment he felt his hands strike a plastic sack.

He ripped the sack out of the sand and tore it open to find what Sangster had called the go package, a black backpack bearing the Polidorium logo at the top. Alex lifted it quickly, looking around as if one of their agents might come to retrieve it at any moment. He opened the pack and found a heavy, leatherlike roll inside. *Like the one Sangster had before, when we were looking for the entrance.* He set it on the ground, rolling it out.

Alex looked down at the gear. He saw a net containing several of the glass water balls, a Polibow with four twelve-bolt cartridges, assorted silver knives, and one of the specially carved, silver-lined stakes. The Polibow had a sling and he slipped it over his shoulder. There was also a sort of air gun with a grappling hook in the barrel. *Cool.* He decided to ignore the Beretta; he had trained with hunting rifles but knew enough about guns to not try using one he'd never been taught. The stake he shoved through a belt loop.

Alex found a Bluetooth headset fastened to the roll, retrieved it, and put it on. He thought back to his time at the farmhouse.

He tapped the button on the headset. He wondered who would answer and prepared several responses.

An answer came across: "Farmhouse."

Alex said, "Farmhouse, I'm in the field, I need Sangster."

Instantly the voice said, "Routing."

Alex blinked, pleased with himself, and waited. There was a series of clicks and finally an answer as Sangster came on the line.

"This is Sangster."

"Sangster, this is Van Helsing."

There was a silence, and then he heard a distant crackle.

"You've got to be kidding me."

"I have the go package," Alex said. "I'm going in." He clicked the device off.

Alex turned toward the water, feeling the corresponding rise of static in his mind. He threw a glass ball into the air, raised the Polibow, and took it down in one shot. The tinkling shards of glass on water opened up another world. Now he had to hurry.

Cold shot through Alex's limbs as he waded into the lake. Near the lip of the tunnel, where the water was up to his chest, it got worse; the temperature plummeted. He could see his breath. His teeth started to chatter as he grabbed the edge of the entrance and swung his leg up, dragging himself onto the stone floor. The static was pounding. This was a place of evil.

Cut that out. Pay attention.

For a moment he remembered his first skiing instructor, on a mountain where Alex had gotten into a precarious spot and had started to complain about whether or not he could make it back down.

What are you doing right now? Are you solving your problem or is this just noise?

For now, the static was just noise. He forced his mind to push the static back and down.

Drenched to the bone, Alex stopped for a moment at the mouth of the tunnel. Inside, the air was still frigid, but at least he wasn't swimming in it anymore. He crouched low, collecting himself. The tunnel itself was as wide as a driveway, and as he looked down, he saw that it sloped at about a 15-degree angle, leveling off out of sight, probably dropping again. *How many underground lairs can this part of Switzerland hold?* He turned over the pack, observing that the zipper worked as a seal, so that the pack was waterproof. Alex touched the tunnel wall. It was made of what seemed to be stone, lined with a matrix that stretched around and down as far as the eye could see. At intervals he saw reinforcing beams embedded with skulls.

He clicked the Bluetooth device on, and said, "You still there?"

"Alex," came Sangster's voice, cool and steady. "You need to turn around. Don't go into that tunnel."

"Too late," said Alex. "You gonna help me or are we going to discuss this a little more?"

"You're in danger already."

"Yeah, so I need your help," he said. Alex needed to

have some idea of what he was dealing with. "The walls are lined with a white—like a white net. What is this stuff?" The matrix glimmered in the light as Alex ran his hand along it.

Sangster responded, "That is probably a reinforcing mesh of bone."

"Ugh," Alex said, pulling his hand back.

"Not pure bone, though, there's probably metal or something in it. It's a polymer of some kind."

"Vampires make polymers?"

"Vampires make work orders," Sangster said. "Probably someone else would make the polymer."

"I never knew they were that organized," Alex said. *Of course, I never knew they existed.* There was a flicker behind him at the mouth of the tunnel, and he turned with surprise—only to see the opening closing up. Now a sheen of water lay across the top, and he could make out the distant moon shining, murky through the liquid.

Alex walked back to the entrance and struck the wall of water, wanting to know what he was dealing with. His hand bounced off painfully, smarting as if he had struck concrete. "Ow!"

"What?" Sangster hissed, far away.

"I smacked the entrance," Alex said. "It's closed. So

would this be technology or magic?"

"Both," Sangster replied. Alex could hear the teacher deciding he had no choice but to guide him. "Okay. Alex, you need to *keep moving*. You can't stay still very long. Stay away from the walls. I'm thinking they're not sensitive or you'd probably be hearing alarms already, but you don't want to take any chances."

Alex snatched his hand away from the wall. "You could warn me about these things ahead of time."

"You're telling me," the teacher said. "What about your . . . other sense?"

Alex blinked. "It's vibrating and, you know, there."

"I was afraid of that," said Sangster. "You won't be able to use your sense to warn you of a sneak attack because right now you're surrounded by evil. It's just going to constantly clang. We'll find someone to help you with that."

Alex wondered who they could find to help. "That someone wouldn't be my own father, would it?"

"I think that's up to you," Sangster said.

As Alex crept, Sangster whispered advice to Alex, *Just stay low. Don't go anywhere wide-open. If you see anyone coming after you, run. You're there to find the hostages and information, not to engage the enemy.*

After he had traveled about a half mile, the light had

grown so dim that Alex spoke again. "It's getting hard to see."

"Do you have the go package?"

"Yes."

"Reach in and feel for the left pocket. You'll find Velcroed to the side a pair of infrared glasses. Put them on."

Alex found them. They were lightweight, barely bulkier than a welder's mask, and when Alex had slipped them on, he found the button on the side and pressed.

Suddenly he could see again. He nearly screamed.

Sangster heard him gasp. Alex said, "I found someone."

"A guard?"

"No."

Two inches from Alex's face was a *cage.* It hung right in front of him, a swinging birdcage about six feet tall, suspended from the ceiling. A leering, mummified skull lay at eye level with him on the floor of the cage, crumpled with the bones. The skeleton wore green and tattered clothing.

"Easy," Sangster whispered.

"What the . . . ?" Alex slowly edged around the cage, moving to the center of the drive. He took in the crumpled form—it wore, *he* wore heavy boots, baggy pants, and a canvas belt.

"It's a skeleton, or nearly a skeleton, in a hanging cage," he said. "It's dressed like someone from a World War Two movie." He crouched a bit to see the breast of the skeleton, and read its name aloud. "Bates. Why is this here?"

"It's probably a warning," Sangster said. "Don't get distracted, just keep moving."

Breathe. Keep moving. Alex began to edge past the skeleton.

And then it woke up.

A rattling hiss erupted from the thin, mummified lips as the dead, dry eyes within the skull focused on him. A bony arm shot out of the cage as Alex passed, grabbing his jacket.

"Yahh!" Alex tried to twist away, and the bony hand gripped harder—its fingers were partially in his pocket. "It's alive, it's got me!"

Time froze for a second as Alex felt himself being tugged toward the cage, the nearly clean skull gnashing its teeth at him. The skull was beginning to moan. *Wait. Wait.* He had the Polibow in his hands.

"Bash it," said Sangster evenly, only the slightest hint of whatever concern he must be feeling. "Get free."

Alex swung the Polibow down against the thing's wrist

and felt it crack and fall away, clattering back against the cage. He panted and stepped back farther down the corridor, staring as the skeleton kept pawing futilely at him from within his cage.

"I'm free," he said.

The skeleton was still moaning.

"That's a zombie moan," Sangster said insistently.

"I know! It's a freaking zombie skeleton in a freaking—"

"It's going to call others."

"What?"

"Turn around," said Sangster.

Slowly Alex turned, as the sound of unearthly, guttural moaning began to pour from the dark tunnel beyond.

Through his infrared glasses he could see the forms begin to shamble away from coffers in the wall—shuffling corpses, slowly moving toward him. Zombies.

"Oh my God," Alex said.

"How many are there?"

"I see six," Alex said.

"They'll be slow and stupid," Sangster said rapidly. "Try to move past them. Don't let them grab you. If you have to kill one, a head shot is your only choice."

The zombies moved slowly, forming a helter-skelter line across the tunnel. "I don't see a space to get through."

Sangster paused for a second. "Pick the tallest one, bend low, run fast, and hit him below the knees. Keep running."

Alex nodded even though Sangster couldn't see him. The zombies coming toward him were four males and two females, some in civilian clothing. One was wearing a kilt.

A soldier zombie in the middle was tallest, still wearing its World War II helmet, its skeletal head tilted sideways. Alex bent low and ran.

The dull stench of old decay hit his nose as Alex's shoulder struck the zombie at the knees. The two zombies on either side saw him coming, staring mindlessly and pawing at him as their fellow tumbled over. Alex rolled past and then started to scramble up, but his foot slipped on the slick stone of the tunnel. He sprawled out.

The zombie he had plowed under was still lying facedown, confused, but the ones on either side were tracking Alex. When he slipped, his foot came close to one of them and a long, bony arm grabbed his ankle. The zombie, a man in a parka, opened its mouth and moaned.

Alex tried to rise but the zombie began to drag him.

Alex raised the Polibow, aiming for the head. He fired a bolt and hit the zombie in the shoulder. It staggered, still pulling. Alex was sliding on his back. He fired again, catching the zombie in the head this time, and it fell back, dead. Another lunged and this time Alex was ready, bringing the Polibow up and close to the zombie's forehead, firing.

Alex got up. The others were still coming; the one he had tripped had managed to flip over and get up. Alex began to run, and felt a crunch beneath his feet as he went. He kept running as the moans persisted.

Think. They're coming steadily. If he wanted to sneak into the school and rescue his friends, he had to deal with them or they'd follow him the whole way. Other creatures, smarter creatures, could hear them at any second.

Alex stopped as the four remaining zombies came toward him. He looked at the Polibow. He had five shots left.

He picked a zombie, ran toward it, and pumped a bolt into its head before the others could grab him. He turned around and took out the second.

The third, slow moving but insistent, grabbed him by the jacket. Alex took the zombie by the wrist and spun it against the wall. He raised the Polibow and fired, dropping the zombie.

One more, but it was close—it was on him, jaws snap-ping and moaning. Alex fired, missing, the bolt zing-ing into the distance. *One left.* Then he would have to reload, and that would mean opening the pack. *Make it count.* The zombie came close, mouth open wide. Alex put the Polibow between its teeth and drove a bolt up into its brain.

He stepped back. He was alone.

Very alone. He had dropped, and crushed, the Bluetooth.

CHAPTER 18

In for a dime, in for a dollar. There was no going back. The tunnel stretched another quarter mile before turning a corner. After that, Alex took off the infrared glasses, because he could make out a glow of light in the distance.

When he reached the end of the tunnel and crouched at the entrance of a vast expanse beyond, Alex let out a low, barely audible whistle.

This was the Scholomance.

Look at the size of that thing. He had never seen a cave this huge in his life, even compared with the Polidorium headquarters. It stretched seemingly for miles, the shimmering white mesh moving all along the interior, keeping it from collapsing. His sensation of danger was immense and everywhere, a dull static in the back of his mind.

Alex surveyed what he could make out.

Before him lay a column of vehicles partially obscuring his view of what must be the main entrance of the school, but also giving him some cover. About two football-field lengths from his position lay a main gate, wide enough for cars. It was tall, iron, and marked with a large S. Starting at the gate was a stone wall, going into the distance on either side.

Past the vehicles and past the gate, Alex saw a courtyard and a turreted castle beyond. Around and behind the castle lay several large buildings of modern design, black marble and glass, looking very much like modern university structures.

Let's go, Alex thought. He scurried forward and to the side, crouching next to an armored personnel carrier. This was one of the vehicles he had seen coming in the night Icemaker had arrived. What next? He would need to get through the gate or over the wall. Beyond that, what? He was a human in jeans and a light jacket. He would need to find some way to pass.

Next to the cold metal of the personnel carrier, Alex surveyed for guards. No one stood between him and the wall. He took a breath, rose, and sprinted the distance, not stopping until he laid his hands on the stone of the wall itself.

The wall was twelve feet high, more than twice his height. Alex studied it. For a moment he considered running to the gate and shimmying up between the gate and the wall, but it was too risky. He would be exposed the whole time.

Then Alex remembered the go package. He slipped off the pack, crouching low next to the wall, and pulled out the grappling gun. *While I'm at it* . . . He put a fresh cartridge in the Polibow and closed the pack.

He stepped back, aiming the grappling gun in the air, and fired. A quiet *shoomp* sound sent a silver hook and braided climbing line high and over the wall. Alex pulled until he heard it clank softly on the other side. He waited till it had found purchase on the lip of the wall and then tugged.

Within moments Alex climbed up and lay flat on the top of the wall. It was rough-hewn but not razor sharp. He found he could press his face against it without too much discomfort, and he froze there, watching. Then he gingerly, quickly drew in the line, bundled it up, and slipped it back in the pack as he surveyed the scene.

The grass was *white*, he realized with astonishment.

Where on a normal campus there would be manicured green lawns, here the grass was bone white and nearly blinding, thick and neatly trimmed. The "sky," which was the distant rock ceiling of the cavern, only contributed to the bizarre nature of the landscape.

Then he saw guards milling around near the gate. He ducked his head, feeling adrenaline flood through his chest. He would have been right next to them if he had chosen that path.

They were dressed all in white, like the girl he had faced in the woods barely a week ago. He thought for a second. That was before Icemaker got here. And Icemaker's vampires had worn red.

Now he realized how he would get in. But he wouldn't want these. *These* were the locals, guards of the Scholomance. They would probably be more recognizable—he would have a harder time replacing one. The red guards were newcomers and would be barely known.

Alex waited for the guards to move farther off, then began to creep along the top of the wall until he reached an area where more vehicles were parked below him on the inside of the wall.

Near another APC was a pair of vampires in dark red gear and hoods. Perfect.

This didn't happen: He didn't drop off the wall and tap the vampires on the shoulder. The vampires didn't look back like a pair of idiots and let Alex clobber them and take their clothes. That *might* have happened—in an infinite universe that had to happen sometimes—but it didn't happen this time, because Alex nearly blew it falling off the wall.

Alex started to drop, but as he swept his legs down his sweatshirt caught on the jagged top of the brick, and he gasped as it caught his neck. He pushed off and gasped again as he landed on his shoulder.

Fifteen yards away, the two vampires in red swept their heads instantly in his direction.

Spotted. He didn't have time for anything else. The vampires moved with insane speed, a blur of red leggings and boots and white faces coming toward him. Alex lifted the Polibow and squeezed off a bolt. With a *fwoosh* the vampire on the right went up in a cloud of dust.

The other went straight for Alex, grabbing him by the throat before he had a chance to register what was happening. The Polibow fell from Alex's hand and for a moment Alex stared into the vampire's shining eyes. "What's this?" hissed the vampire.

Alex blinked as time slowed to a crawl.

Never freeze. Answer the questions.

What's going on? He's choking me.

What do you have? I dropped my weapon!

What else do you have? I have a stake, it's in my belt.

The vampire's nails were digging into his neck as he found the handle of the stake in his belt loop, no more hesitation, *grab it.*

It had eyes. Human eyes. Eyes on a body someone gave birth to once. Someone . . .

This isn't a person. It's a nonperson, a former person, a post-critical-failure-whatever person. Stab it before it makes you one, too. Do it now.

He yanked the stake up, catching the vampire in the belly. The creature hissed in pain as his skin burned, flesh sizzling as it touched the wooden shaft, and he dropped Alex.

Alex wasted no time in withdrawing the weapon and slamming it home again into the creature's chest. The dust explosion scattered over him and Alex's eyes blazed with agony as the particles got in them. He bent forward, blinking, feeling the plastic of his contacts swimming frantically over his eyeballs.

Alex breathed hard, blinking.

Great. It would help if you got the clothes before you burned them up.

He moved in silence along the line of vehicles until he found another chance—a red-uniformed vampire working under the hood of a Humvee.

The static started to hiss more loudly as he pressed on, his heart racing. *You can do this. Go.*

Alex ran up and smacked aside the bar holding up the hood. With all his strength he brought the hood down on the creature. It landed heavily, trapping the vampire's head. The vampire fought, clawing but unseeing.

Alex slammed the hood again and the vampire went still.

It couldn't be dead, he realized. It didn't go *fwoosh*.

He felt his blood pumping as he moved quickly, as if by instinct. No—certainly by instinct. This was the business he was built for. Alex grabbed the vampire's tunic and dared to lift the vehicle hood slightly as he ripped the tunic up and over the creature's head. He let the hood drop again and made quick work of stripping the red leggings, boots, and tunic from the creature. Just as the vampire was coming to, he shot it.

Alex ducked behind the Humvee and donned the red leggings and tunic over his own clothes—they were much too big for him—and was forced to wear the backpack underneath, over his shirt. He kept the Polibow on his shoulder under the tunic as well, but slid the stake into an outer pocket of the leggings.

By the time he reached the end of the vehicle line, he was dressed like a vampire, albeit not a tall one, and hoping his hood helped him look like one.

Alex paused at the edge of the castle. He could see the whole courtyard and a number of large, black marble buildings behind the Scholomance castle. For the first time he got a good view of the populace.

There were vampires on the lawn before the castle and around the side as well, some walking together, some sprawled on the straight, white grass with what Alex surmised were books. Some of the books he saw were old and leather-bound, but many of them were new and slick.

There were vampires playing soccer in the main court-yard. This place looked like a university mall or park, and the whole student body seemed to be out and about. He had no choice but to step forward, hood drawn over his head, and begin walking quickly along the path, moving up alongside the castle, looking for an entrance.

As he walked, a pair of vampires in white looked his way, and Alex nodded as best he could in his hood, hoping the mortality of his flesh did not show or smell through the borrowed tunic.

If Paul and Minhi were being held captive, surely they

would be in a dungeon. That would be in the castle. But he didn't see a side entrance into the castle.

As he reached the rear of the castle, he saw that it was connected to the black marble buildings. An entrance ahead of him, into the next building, read simply CAFETERIA.

Well, vampires gotta eat. Or drink. He tried not to think too hard about it, because there was no turning back and he had to keep moving.

Alex proceeded up a short staircase, through glass doors, and into a cafeteria like none he had ever seen.

Oh my God. There were tables throughout the room, with a familiar hodgepodge of students studying and talking, but next to term papers and books and mash notes were glasses, goblets, plastic Nalgene bottles, all filled with a red liquid. Alex didn't want to contemplate *how* they filled the vessels, but then he saw them: captives. Lining the back of the cafeteria were cages hanging from hooks in the ceiling. In the cages were humans, sullen and unseeing.

Fear shot through him for Minhi and Paul. He scanned the captives' faces rapidly as he drew closer, moving along the edge of the cafeteria. There were seven, all told. The half-dead captives were as pale as death but alive, dressed shabbily in hospital gowns. Four females, three males, all adult. Paul and Minhi were not among them.

As he passed, one of the captives, a woman who appeared to be about forty, looked at him, and his heart leapt as she seemed to move her mouth.

He had to keep going.

Alex made a decision that he knew was only awaiting the right moment. He exited the cafeteria on the right and made his way into a hallway.

A hallway that was full of vampires.

CHAPTER 19

For a moment the static rose to a roar and he had to pause and force it to the back of his mind.

A crowd of vampires, most of them wearing white, was moving steadily toward him from either direction, passing all around, each headed his or her own way. Alex turned to the wall, pretending to study a bulletin board, looking for a map.

There wasn't one. For a moment he listened to the voices as they passed, hearing the vampires talking among themselves. He could pick up nothing of import—most of them seemed to be students concerned about classes. Here and there he heard the term *Icemaker*, but nothing he could grab on to.

Then he heard voices on a higher register and looked down the hall. A bunch of student vampires, appearing to be in their mid-teens, were moving in a group. They were young ones—or at least vampires who had been young when turned.

A tall vampire woman with long, brown hair came out of the cafeteria and seemed to stop and look at Alex as she passed, slowing a bit.

Determined not to stand still, Alex waited until the classroom-size group had nearly passed and then he slipped in behind them.

For about fifty yards he walked with the short vampires. One toward the end of the line looked back and slowed to walk next to him.

It was a vampire boy with black hair and white eyes, his hood down. "Are you one of Icemaker's army?" he asked.

Alex kept walking, nodding inside his hood. "Yes," he rasped. "We, ah, serve the master in all things."

"Do you all talk like that? That must be really weird. I thought only the really ancient ones talked that way. Are you very old but got changed as a boy?"

Alex looked sideways, trying not to let too much of his face show. "I don't remember anymore," he said. *Ridiculous answer.*

His eye started to twitch. He felt instantly what was happening and swore inwardly. A speck of dust fell from his eyelash into his right eye and he blinked rapidly. "I mean, it was very long ago," he stuttered to the boy. He tried to control his blinking, but the soft plastic of the contact was shifting under his eyelid. It was losing its grasp on his eyeball. Beside him, the boy was trying to get a better look at him as he kept talking.

"I'm kind of new at this—I only got changed recently," the boy said. "But I'm getting better. Some of us are going to sneak out later and go hunting."

Alex said, choking back the itch in his eye, "Hunting?"

"Absolutely," said the boy. "But don't tell anyone. One girl didn't come back after we hunted this painter the other night. It's against the rules, you know. But still."

"But still," Alex repeated. *Don't let him see your face. Don't touch your face.* The contact rolled in his eyelid as he blinked uncontrollably and felt it pop out.

He was blind in the right eye. Half his vision, including the boy, went into a dull, indecipherable blur.

He panicked for a second; he hated being blind, he couldn't be blind here, not now. The contact hadn't fallen—he felt it resting on his cheek, slick and stuck for a moment.

"You know, you kind of smell funny," the vampire boy said.

Get away. He shrugged as a response to the boy, reaching inside his pocket for the stake and dropping back.

The crowd was moving toward the next corner, but on his left, in his clear vision, Alex spotted a large, black door along the hallway. He prayed that the contact would stay stuck to his face if he just moved steadily enough. As he passed the door, he slid in one quick movement to the wall, grasped the brass handle, and opened the door, slipping out of the hall into a room.

He immediately grabbed the contact, knowing his hands were filthy but having no other choice, and hurriedly popped the lens into his mouth. He kept it on his tongue, willing himself not to swallow, not to allow his mouth to fill too much with saliva. He could wash it with his tongue if he was careful enough.

Alex looked around and nearly gulped in surprise.

The room was entirely made of gold—actual, literal gold, with a golden slab at the center. Instantly he saw that the slab was not resting on any support; it floated in the air as if suspended from invisible wire. Something the size of a birdcage, two feet tall and rounded at the top, sat on the slab, covered in a golden blanket.

Alex kept his mouth shut, tumbling the contact

lens around on his tongue as he spun back. The door behind him appeared as a thinly demarcated line engraved in a wall that shimmered in gold as well. The walls shone and went on in a circle. *No right angles. No decoration.*

Fix your eye.

Alex furiously rubbed his hands as clean as he could get them on the tunic, swishing the contact against the roof of his mouth. After a moment he stuck out his tongue, grasping the lens tenderly between his right thumb and forefinger.

He held it up, using his good left eye to visually inspect the outline of the contact. Alex frowned—he had it turned inside out. It didn't look like a bowl. The curve of the contact lens was lipped out at the edges. Alex popped it back into his mouth and moved his tongue, feeling it switch its orientation. He stuck out his tongue again and grabbed it.

Alex looked close with his good eye. The contact was mottled with spit, but unblemished and whole. He pried open his right eye and pressed the contact in, wincing as he swirled his eye around, letting the lens settle back into place. After a moment he was able to blink. *Man, I hate these things.*

Alex swiveled in a circle. *What is this place?*

The birdcage with the blanket stared back at him in silence.

He had no choice. He had to see.

Slowly, stepping on a soft golden floor that was burnished to an extreme shine, Alex approached the slab. As he drew near he became aware of a dull thrumming sound.

Alex reached for the blanket, watching his own human hand as if stunned that he dared. He grabbed the top of the blanket and ripped it back.

Before him lay the world.

It spun slowly in the air, the vaguely misshapen world itself. As Alex peered closer he saw that this was not simply a globe—it *was* the earth, in some magical way. He saw textures and crevices, vast swaths of white concrete stretching through North America, glass and steel towering in the Northeast.

He circled the globe, tracing the line of the Great Wall of China through Asia.

There were golden dots shining from the globe, groups of them in Europe, America, Asia, everywhere.

He circled a second time against the slow revolution of the earth, peering closely at Europe, trying to find Switzerland.

A large glob of gold shone from Lake Geneva.

This was a map of vampires. In his mind he remembered the slogan of the Polidorium: *There are such things.*

Alex reached out a finger to touch the Atlantic.

It felt wet to the touch and he scoffed lightly. Then the room erupted with alarms.

As blaring horns rang out, Alex threw the blanket back over the vampire earth and bolted for the door. He pushed at it, and in a second was out in the hallway.

The door slid back into place, looking no more impressive than it had before.

He took a half second to study the hall and saw now that fewer vampires were passing. Out here, he couldn't hear the alarm. He kept moving.

Down the hall Alex stopped at another bulletin board with little note cards that read things like MUSICAL TRYOUTS and NEED A ROOMMATE/NONSMOKING ONLY. He turned his hood to the wall to lessen the exposure of his face to the passing students.

On one side of the board was a calendar with upcoming and current events listed, and Alex silently read them off.

His eyes landed on a notice that filled him with alarm: MIDNIGHT TONIGHT: PRESENTATION OF THE KEYHOLE SACRIFICE. DUNGEON AUDITORIUM. ALL WELCOME.

Keyhole sacrifice?

Keyhole?

His mind raced. There was something Sid had said, something Mary Shelley had put into *Frankenstein* when she revised it. Mary Shelley said Polidori had told a story about a skull-headed lady looking through a keyhole. And Sid had said that was made up, because Polidori was working on a story about *Byron*. Alex shook his head, wishing he could get Sid on his useless Bluetooth to talk him through it. Too many coincidences. Was it possible that somehow *Frankenstein* carried a clue?

Alex snuck a look at his watch: 11:42 P.M.

He had to move.

In the corner of the bulletin board Alex saw a campus map. *The Dungeon Auditorium.* He found its location and headed for the interior of the castle back the way he'd come.

Alex walked as quickly as he dared through the hallways, passing the golden map room and the cafeteria, until he entered darker, older interiors. The tile of the new buildings gave way to the rough-hewn stone of the castle. He joined a steady flow of vampires all heading in the same direction. Alex reached an open door into a circular stairwell that traveled down several flights. No one was paying attention to him as he descended, and after a moment he understood why. As he reached a large entryway where many vampires were entering, he felt the temperature drop mightily.

He pushed silently into an auditorium, past rows and rows of seats that were filling up.

Toward the front, with a backdrop of curtains, was a tower of ice that flattened out at the top into a circular raised stage. From the stage of ice rose a tombstonelike monolith, also ice, some ten feet high.

In the center of the monolith was a window, cut in the shape of a keyhole and framed by stone set into the ice. Before it stood Icemaker himself.

Alex stuck to the wall, reaching the corner and trying to melt into it. The lights dimmed.

"My children, what is your suit?" came the voice of Icemaker.

"We seek everlasting life," the crowd responded.

"The time has come to become something new," he said. "To speak to the demon-goddess Nemesis and beg her for our queen. All has been prepared."

He held up a scroll. Alex stared at it, the carved animal head atop it—a fox? "In a few minutes' time, at the start of what the mortals call the Feast of Our Lady of Sorrows"—Icemaker looked up at the enormous clock, which read ten to midnight—"we will summon her and make our sacrifice." He gestured dramatically toward the curtains in the back of the auditorium.

The crowd roared in approval.

Minhi and Paul had not been among the captives at the cafeteria. They were probably about to be the main course here. That meant they might be backstage even now. Alex started moving along the wall.

CHAPTER 20

Minhi awoke in the dark and had no idea what time it was. For the first several hours of her captivity she had wrestled, she had pleaded and screamed. Then had come the—how best to call it? That pep rally of the damned? And since that moment she had sat in her cage, waiting, watching.

Now she could hear a great gathering in the auditorium and *he* was speaking again.

A great, thick curtain had been drawn on the backstage, so that she and Paul were hidden, as though awaiting the applause that would open the curtains once more.

Minhi was not accepting her fate. She was accepting

only that she lacked immediate options. Fate was far from decided.

Paul, meanwhile, had also awoken and was now pressing his back against the bars and trying to break the cage open.

"Are you really trying that again?" Minhi asked.

Paul dropped back to the floor of his cage. "I have to try *something*."

"We'll get a chance to try something," said Minhi, "but it'll happen when there's a change."

"What do you mean, a change?"

"Listen to that," she said, indicating the muffled noise of what sounded like a call-and-response meeting. "I mean, we're not going to sit here forever. They're going to have to move us eventually."

"I have news for you; that will not be a good time for us."

"But," she said, "that's when lots of things will happen. Locks will be unlocked, and so on. It won't be easy, but we might have a chance then."

Paul looked at Minhi. "So how do we deal with them?"

Minhi was thinking. "What do we know about vampires?" she said, daring to use the word neither seemed comfortable with. "They're strong, for one thing, like superhero strong." She sounded like she was making a list.

"They don't like sunlight," Paul said. "In those movies Sid makes me watch, the vampire always gets burnt up when the sunlight hits him."

"That's in movies," Minhi said. "We don't know if that's true. I mean, for instance, in movies nobody ever has caller ID or cell phones that work. Do *you* have a cell that works, by the way?"

"Not down here. Are you suggesting that the movies are not a guide for life?" Paul asked. "Whatever will I do now?"

Minhi smirked. "Okay, so that's an idea, though—if we can trick them into the sunlight—"

A sour, female voice hissed, "That only works *sometimes*."

Minhi looked up in horror as a female vampire dropped silently from the rafters to the floor.

She had spiky yellow hair and white robes that fluttered as she descended. She looked no more than sixteen, but Minhi knew that vampires tended to measure their years in decades or even centuries. The vampire girl began to walk in front of the cages. Her bone white skin almost glowed in the dim light behind the stage.

"What's the game we're playing, chiclets? How to kill

a vampire? You can forget sunlight—the old ones can handle it—and anyway, you're about two miles underground, sweetheart."

"Who are you?" Minhi demanded.

"My name's Elle," she said.

"So sun doesn't burn you?" asked Paul, defiant.

Elle raised an eyebrow and came close to Paul's cage, showing her fangs. "Burn? Me? I'm not telling. Not as much as I'll bet *you* do; you're paler than Casper—but maybe that's just fear."

"What do you want?" Minhi asked.

"I'm watching over you," the vampire answered, "until the moment you're needed."

Elle took a moment to study them silently, and then she spoke again. The lusty look in Elle's eye suggested that she yearned to devour them herself.

Elle licked her lips, looking back and forth, then said, "Let's play another game."

Minhi crouched, watching, as Elle continued, "You've made me really curious about how much you all know, so I'm going to ask each of you a question: *myth* or *reality*."

"About what?" asked Paul.

"About vampires!" Elle shook her head in disbelief that Paul would even ask. "Vampires are like Americans, we *love* to talk about ourselves. Myth or reality?"

Paul asked, "What do we win if we get it right?"

"You get to live," she snarled.

Minhi felt her eyes grow wide but she controlled her fear. "Oh, now, I know we're here for something more than that. Sounded to me like your fearless vampire leader wants to use us for something else. I'll bet his instructions were pretty clear."

Elle looked thoughtful. "It's amazing, you know; I have the *hardest* time with clear instructions." She went back to Paul's cage. Paul sat there with his arms folded, looking down, and she crouched to his level. "Man, you're a big dude," she offered. "You'll be like two sacrifices' worth of sacrifice. You're like a supersize sacrifice. Myth or reality, big guy." She leaned in. "Vampires can *fly*."

Paul stared at her. Minhi started to whisper something and Elle turned around, holding up a shiny black fingernail. "No helping!"

Paul looked around him, then said, "Myth."

"Not bad." Elle stood up. "That's another tough one, so I would have accepted 'it depends,' because there are some special cases."

She went back to Minhi's cage. Elle poked her through the bars. "Hey. Myth or reality?"

"Come on . . ."

"Vampires are burned by crosses."

Minhi shut her eyes, then said, "Reality."

"Wow," Elle said. "Usually everyone gets that wrong these days. Yeah. Holy stuff burns like crazy; go figure." She walked back to Paul.

"This game is totally not fair," Paul spat.

"Why?" Elle asked, amused.

"Because we've seen everything in movies, and it's all different from movie to movie."

"Well, then why don't you just restrict yourself to answers that reflect *reality*. Myth or reality: Vampires have to sleep in coffins."

Minhi watched Paul catch this question and stop. He backed up, his eyes flying back and forth. Elle waited a few seconds, then put her hands on the bars, leaning toward him, her long black nails glistening in the dimness. "Well?"

"Myth."

Elle reached out her arm and grazed a fingernail along Paul's cheek. "Very good. Mounds of earth, yes—but there's nothing special about a coffin. Some of the old-timers still like them, though."

Elle moved again to Minhi. "That brings me back to you. Myth or reality."

"That's a stupid name," Minhi said. "It sounds like Truth or Dare, like you're asking me to choose. I'll do a myth, please."

"Myth or reality," Elle said, wagging her finger. "Vampires can fall in love."

Minhi stared for a long moment. "Reality."

Elle clicked her tongue. "Ohh. No, no. Obsession, but not love. It's just not there. It's all burned out. No pity, no empathy. You'd be surprised how much you don't miss that."

Then, like a snake striking, Elle reached out, her steely fingers grabbing Minhi by the neck, dragging her to the front of her cage. Minhi was clawing at Elle's pale arm and Elle hissed as her nails started to draw along Minhi's neck.

"So let me ask you something," came the voice of Alex Van Helsing.

Elle gasped and stared up into the rafters. Minhi twisted away from Elle as Alex dropped to the floor.

Alex continued, "Do you *paint* those nails black, or is that just a bonus that comes with the fangs?"

On the platform, Icemaker stood, the curtains behind him, vampire guards on either side.

"Now you will witness destiny," he cried, and he

reached out his hand, his eyes on the keyhole. With one razor-sharp thumb he cut his hand, and soon a glittering kind of blood, his own cursed clan lord ichor, dripped down into the circle before him, flowing in grooves carved in the ice.

"This blood is not mortal blood," said he. "It is not the blood you remember." And he continued:

"*Ye know what I have known; and without power*
I could not be amongst ye: but there are
Powers deeper still beyond—I come in quest
Of such, to answer unto what I seek."

After a moment a whisper came, lighting on the frozen air. Frost rose and swirled, up to the keyhole window, swirling in the stone and then bursting out. And then the demon Nemesis herself appeared, robed and winged, a glowing goddesslike humanoid form of clouds and ice. Her eyes were a deep void.

The demon said:

"*Prostrate thyself, and thy condemned clay,*
Child of the Earth! or dread the worst."

Icemaker smiled. And stood, coming to his full height before the circle. He looked the demon in the void eyes and said, "I know it, and yet ye see I kneel not."

"Thou art changed," said Nemesis. "What wouldst thou?"

Icemaker beheld the grooves and said, "This is not the blood of a mortal, nor the blood of a lowly undead. It is the ichor of a lord, of one who has been tinged with that of the ancients. I make a sacrifice to receive what I desire."

"And what is it that you desire?" responded the demon.

"At this proper time, at this hour of the Feast of Our Lady of Sorrows, I wish power over life and death," he said, "beginning with my beloved, Claire."

In the air the vampire formed a small image, a cameo of ice and blood that he held in his hand: Claire, treacherous mistress, mother of a child he had taken and then had taken from him, bearer of a love he no longer felt except as obsession.

Icemaker threw the cameo of blood and ice into the flowing grooves, and it hissed.

"Let it be done," said Nemesis.

Backstage, Alex recognized the vampire he faced. It was the girl who had been spying on him through his window, who had thrown him onto the roof. The glimmering bolt flew through the air, grazing the top of Elle's shoulder. Elle stumbled back.

"How did you know about me?" he demanded, firing again. This bolt impacted with her shoulder and drove her back, sticking her to the wall.

"You?" she spat. "We've been *waiting* for one of you."

Alex turned for a brief second to the cages. Minhi and Paul shrank back until Alex pulled down his hood, revealing his face.

Paul suddenly burst out laughing.

"What?" Alex asked.

Paul said, "I'm sorry, it's just kind of 'aren't you a little short to be a stormtrooper?' "

Alex protested, "You should know I got silver bolts right here that—" and then Elle ripped away from the wall, slamming into him, knocking him sideways.

He struck the ground, exhaling sharply. He lost hold of the Polibow and the weapon fell. As he landed on his back, the vampire leapt on top of him and grabbed him by the shoulders, rolling back her head, her mouth open. She bared her fangs. Alex watched her whole body start to come forward.

Suddenly she jerked—Minhi had caught her by the hood that dangled behind her neck. Alex grabbed the bow. As he did so, he saw a fire extinguisher and what he would need: an ax.

The vampire growled, turning toward Minhi. Alex aimed and there was a quiet pumping sound of the Polibow, as two wood-threaded silver bolts went toward Elle's chest, but she spun, one of the bolts finding solid purchase in her shoulder, where it burned and hissed loudly. Elle growled and leapt backward, grabbing the curtains. She put all her weight into yanking at them viciously. Golden rings at the top of the rafters began to strain and pop as the curtains swayed. Elle disappeared into the dark rafters above.

Alex ran to the ax on the wall. He returned, moving quickly, tearing apart the locks of the cages and setting Minhi and Paul free. Just as their feet hit the boards they heard a thunderous sound.

The heavy red curtains were swaying violently, more of the rings popping and groaning, and then they gave out, crashing violently to the floor.

Alex, Minhi, and Paul turned to face the wrath of Icemaker and five hundred of his closest friends.

CHAPTER 21

For a moment Alex felt the room spinning as he surveyed his chances. Still holding the ax, he turned immediately, shouting to Minhi and Paul, "This way, through the back." The two started to move, but they were still stiff and couldn't go as fast as he'd like.

A hissing sound had enveloped the room and Alex looked behind him to see the great vampire roar, "You!"

Vampires were leaping past the ice tower toward the stage. Alex fired the Polibow, taking one out from twenty yards. "You'll never get out of here alive!" Icemaker bellowed.

As Alex ran through the back, past tall wardrobe

boxes, looking for a door, he heard Paul next to him.

"Where are we going, mate?"

"I have no idea. I'm making it up as I go along," Alex said, before his eyes landed on a rear door. "There."

Paul and Minhi were getting faster, spurred forward by the sound of vampire legs resounding behind them. The door was heavy and steel, and as he pushed down on the exit lever, Alex had an idea.

When they burst through and into the room beyond, Alex slammed the door shut. "Hold it!"

Paul put all his weight on the door as Alex stepped back, looking at the door. It had opened out and was made of metal. He still held the ax. "Step back," Alex cried. Paul jumped away and Alex brought the ax down solid in the doorjamb, snarling the head of it deep between the door and the doorjamb. It would act as a doorstop, at least for a moment.

The room they were in was clearly intended to support dramatic performance—he saw enormous clothes racks with robes and doublets. Costume swords and knives lay on tables. There were footsteps at the door and Alex ran to an enormous wooden wardrobe and called to Paul and Minhi to help him push it.

The furniture piece was old, with rotting casters on the legs, but they shoved it rapidly and slammed it down before the door. On its side it covered about three and a half feet of the door. It started to wobble as something began slamming against it.

"Is there another door out of this room?" Alex called.

"I see one," Minhi said. Alex looked in her direction. There was indeed another door in the rear of the room, next to a stack of paint supplies and backdrop canvases.

The wardrobe shook again. Alex looked at the ax, held there in the door, quivering. "See if they have any paint thinner," he said. "Hurry."

Minhi and Paul ran back to the paint supplies and appeared again with cans of paint thinner, about a gallon each.

"Minhi, find a screwdriver and get the cans open. Paul, help me drag this wardrobe lengthwise." He started pulling the wardrobe away from the door.

Paul paused. "It won't block the door anymore."

"When they get the door open we'll only have a second," Alex said. "It wouldn't stop them anyway. So I'm going to give it to them." They turned the wardrobe so that it lay like a great battering ram on the tile floor, aimed at the door.

Minhi had found a screwdriver on a shelf and was twisting rapidly around the seam of a can as the pounding and yanking on the door increased. "Got it," she said, handing him a can.

The smell of the paint thinner struck his nostrils and burned as Alex sloshed it along the top of the wardrobe and all around it. "Don't let this get on you," he said. For good measure he also sloshed it all over the door.

Then he grabbed the ax handle.

"Okay," Alex said. "I'm gonna pull this ax out, and they're gonna get the door open. And we're gonna push this as far as we can through the doorway. Minhi, when that door opens, throw the other open can."

They both nodded. Paul was studying the thinner. "Do we have a match?"

"We don't need a match."

The pounding increased, hissing audible and loud beyond the metal door. "Okay."

Alex yanked the ax out of the door. He and Paul put their shoulders against the bottom of the wardrobe just as the door started to open. Beyond, in the backstage area, Alex could see hundreds of vampires.

"Minhi, now," Alex said. He saw the other open can of thinner tumble through the air, sloshing backstage among the vampires. They were pushing toward him, stumbling over one another. With all their strength Paul and Alex shoved the wardrobe barely through the door, jamming it into the doorway.

"Step back," Alex said, as he raised the Polibow. There was a vampire coming over the wardrobe, ready to leap at them. He aimed at the heart and fired.

As the vampire pounded his claws on the wardrobe, framed in the doorway, he erupted into flame.

And then the whole wardrobe burst, and beyond the first vampire they could see the next vampire's robes catching fire. A wall of flame shot up as thinner on the floor and curtains and boxes and vampires burst into a raging inferno.

"Let's go," Alex said, and they ran for the back door as the drama prep room itself began to catch fire. Smoke was filling the place. They reached the rear door.

It was locked. Alex brought the ax down on the handle, crushing the lock, and they poured through into a corridor, slamming the door behind them.

Alarms were erupting everywhere, but the corridor they found themselves in was empty. Alex looked back at the door into the drama room. "That fire might not keep them from coming this way; we gotta move."

The three of them ran quickly in the direction Alex chose until they found a stairwell, then up. They headed down the next corridor, doubled back, and went up more stairs.

Paul slapped Alex's shoulder as they came to a stop next to a door. "That was bloody fantastic."

"What is all this?" Minhi indicated the Polibow and the stake. "I thought you said *I* was the action star, but you're practically a manga character."

Alex flushed, catching his breath. "What I lack are the very, very big eyes." He peered out into a hall he recognized. It was the main corridor he'd come down from the cafeteria. As before, there were vampires everywhere, but with the clanging alarms ringing, many of them were looking around in confusion. Some of the Icemaker vampires ran past and disappeared into the distance.

"They're looking for us," Alex said. He pulled on his hood. "But most of them don't know what they're looking for. We're gonna pretend I'm one of them and I've already got you. We'll go out through the cafeteria. It's not far." Alex looked at his friends and said, "I'm going to need to tie you up."

Paul and Minhi stared at him for a moment, but Alex felt instantly for the rope belt around his red tunic. He cut it in half with the sharp edge of one of the Polibow bolts.

"Put 'em out."

"Relax." Paul held out his hands as he looked at Minhi.

"I think I know what he has in mind."

Alex tied the ropes lightly around each of their wrists. "This is meaningless if anyone looks at it carefully," Alex said. "So let's hope no one does." After a moment Alex had his red hood pulled up over his head, and he arranged the two humans in front of him.

"Let me see if I got this," said Minhi as they started to walk. "The two of us are supposed to be your captives."

Alex poked her in the elbow. "Just look morose and defeated. Maybe you were softened up already."

He looked at them both and put his hand on the door. "We're going back among them now. Remember that all people—even vampires, I'm betting—will play along with what seems to be right. So act confident."

"*We're* morose," Paul said. "*You* act confident."

Alex nodded and shoved the door open, moving steadily into the hall.

Once they were in the hall, Alex got behind Minhi and Paul and escorted them as though he did this all the time.

The alarms weren't ringing in the cafeteria. Many vampires were still there, having lunch. Alex moved steadily with his captives. Most of the vampires barely looked as he moved past.

"This is the cafeteria," he said. "We're gonna take a left

through there, out the glass doors on the other side, and onto the lawn."

As they turned to move into the cafeteria, Alex saw two red-garbed vampires coming in their direction. He started shouting at Paul and Minhi and smacked Paul in the back of the head.

"None of thy lip, thou cattle!" *Whack.* "The Dark Lord demands your presence!"

They moved past the two vampires, past more tables. Alex whacked Paul again.

"Hey!" Paul whispered.

"Sorry," Alex said, beneath his hood.

Minhi whispered, "I'm curious where you get this idea that vampires talk like Thor, God of Thunder."

"SILENCE, FOUL COW!"

Minhi looked like she was about to laugh when she caught sight of the other captives, the sad humans in cages along the back wall of the cafeteria. "Oh my God."

"Keep moving," Alex said.

A loud PA system cut on and a woman began to speak.

"ATTENTION."

Paul and Minhi looked back at Alex and he urged them on.

"TWO SACRIFICES HAVE ESCAPED WITH A HUMAN. A REVENANT TRACKER HAS BEEN RELEASED. DO NOT INTERFERE WITH ITS MISSION."

Alex blinked. *A revenant what?*

They were halfway across the cafeteria when they heard a deep, inhuman growl. Alex turned to look at the glass door into the corridor.

A metallic crunch ripped through the air as something blew the door clear off its hinges, sending it clattering across tables.

Amid a wave of glass and ice, a dog the size of a horse burst into the cafeteria. It stopped beyond the door, locking on to Alex and his captives.

No, more than a dog: Its muscular forelegs and haunches were bunched and spiked with shards of what looked like ice instead of fur, and it had a triangular head, like a chow's, allowing maximum leverage and room for teeth. As the dog roared and snapped, Alex saw rows of dripping fangs in its mouth.

The six or seven vampires in the cafeteria looked up and then at Alex, understanding now who he was. One of them, a male, started to run for Alex, and as Alex reached for his Polibow the dog tore right through the vampire in his way, biting it on the shoulder and sending it spinning off into the distance. The other vampires, learning their place, ran.

Alex let Paul and Minhi's rope go, shouting, "Get behind some tables."

With a growl, the dog headed for Alex. He grabbed a table and pushed it over on its side. Dishes and bottles clattered on the floor as he yanked the legs of the table and tried to raise it like a shield. The dog struck the table and sent Alex back, but he held on to the underside.

In his peripheral vision—*thank God I fixed my contacts*—Alex saw Paul and Minhi head for the back glass wall that looked out onto the white lawn. The dog was straddling the table, its paws reaching around it, and one of its claws plunged into the folds of Alex's tunic. As the dog yanked its paw free, Alex felt himself come with it, and then he was flying.

He crashed against the metal roll-down curtain of the large window that separated the kitchen and the cafeteria. The curtain buckled, curling around him as he fell back into the kitchen.

Alex got unsteadily to his feet, looking through the window into the dining hall. Back among the tables, the dog stared at Minhi and Paul for a second, and then steered its head toward Alex. It started running.

Alex turned and slid over a long, stainless steel preparation table, landing next to an industrial convection oven. As he dropped his bow and whipped his tunic off and over his head to gain access to his pack, he caught a glimpse of himself in the oven door. In the glass, the dog cast no reflection. *Life would be better in the glass.*

He picked up the Polibow and the tunic, turned, and ran back toward the metal table just as the dog leapt across the back of the cafeteria and sailed halfway through the window, sticking there for a second. It started snapping wildly as it shoved with its hind legs to push itself through, crumbling and buckling the plaster tiles and the metal pane of the window.

Taking the tunic in his hands, Alex got up on the table and jumped, landing on the creature's shoulders. Shards of ice drove into his leggings and thighs.

The revenant tracker growled angrily, bucking, coming through the window, as Alex brought the tunic down around its head. He wrapped the tunic several times and fell away as the dog burst free of the window. It lurched blindly into the kitchen, sending the table flying.

The dog's triangular head was snapping under the cloth. Alex saw the cloth starting to give way, the creature's harsh, snaking tongue trying to punch through. Alex brought up his bow and shot once at the breast of the creature, but the bolt barely connected as the dog started to run around the kitchen, sending utensils and tables flying. The steel food prep table nearly smashed into Alex's head.

Alex dropped back to the corner and rifled through his pack. He had silver knives. He was going to have to make this personal.

Alex grabbed a pair of the knives and rose, heading to the back of the kitchen, near the oven. "Here," he said, "here, boy!"

The dog's covered head whipped toward him and it leapt, and as it hit the air Alex saw the cloth of the tunic tear free. Its mouth was open as it slammed into the oven, crushing the oven door inward and lodging its head there.

For a second the dog was trapped. As the creature began scrambling for footing on the stainless steel, Alex drew close.

He only had a moment. He watched the muscles underneath the shards of ice that made up its fur. He thrust the first knife deep between the grooves of its fur, up into its breast.

Then he took the other knife and slammed it home.

The dog yelped, and Alex pulled out a glass ball of holy water and smashed it up into the wound.

A hissing sound and bubbling fire began to churn

beneath the icy skin. Alex didn't wait to watch. He was running out of the kitchen as the dog erupted, sending splotches of ice and flame through the cafeteria.

Alex found Minhi and Paul and ran up to them, pushing open the glass cafeteria doors. There were footsteps coming from the corridor, but smoke kept them from seeing how many might be coming.

"Across the lawn," Alex shouted. They made it out onto the white grass and ran for the wall.

There was a crashing sound as the glass doors of the cafeteria burst open again. A tall, bald vampire in red burst out, followed by three security guards. The bald vampire was pointing at Alex and the captives.

"That's the human, he's taking the sacrifices!"

Alex, Minhi, and Paul ran faster, Alex pulling in front. "Follow me," he shouted. As he ran, he extracted the Polibow.

They made a beeline for the vehicles near the wall, but just as they were nearing them, two red-clad vampires came bounding fast toward the trio.

Alex waited until the first one was practically at his throat before firing, shooting a bolt into its chest and sending it *fwooshing* off. The other went straight for Minhi, but Alex saw her meet it, prepared. As the creature went for her throat, she feinted to the side, striking it in the shoulder and sending it flying past her. Paul and Minhi kept moving, but Alex stopped and aimed, catching the vampire in the back—not deep enough. The creature turned and kept pursuing them.

"There, there, that vehicle," Alex said, whipping his arm around as he, Minhi, and Paul ran toward an armored personnel carrier about the size of a school bus.

There was a driver in the front who looked at them and hissed. Alex brought up his weapon and pumped a silver bolt into the creature's chest. Dust and flame erupted and evaporated.

Alex climbed in, dropping his backpack into the passenger seat. Looking out the windshield, he saw it was heavy and threaded with a grid of shining metal. As Minhi and Paul piled in, Alex turned the key and the truck rumbled to life. Minhi came forward, leaning on the driver's seat. "Do you drive?"

Alex put the APC in reverse and started backing up. The pursuing vampires were up on them and Alex grabbed a large, bulbous handle, slamming the side doors closed. "We had a farm in Oklahoma for a while; I've done a little driving there."

"Driving what?"

"Hay, bales of hay," Alex said, and now he put the

vehicle in drive and hit the gas, lurching forward.

They pulled out and Alex aimed right for the vampires, led by the tall bald one. One went under the wheels, the vehicle lurching and shaking as it went over the creature.

"Paul! Minhi!" Alex shouted as he got a handle on the enormous steering wheel. His legs were just long enough to allow him to work the pedals.

"What?" Paul called.

"Look around for what we have in this thing, weapons, rope, anything."

"Alex," Minhi said.

"Yep."

"Why are we driving toward the castle?"

"We're not driving toward the castle," Alex corrected. They rounded the corner of the castle and now were hurtling along the wall. "We're driving toward the cafeteria."

"What?" Paul cried. "Are you bloody insane? We just got out of there."

Alex took a second to check himself. Nope, not insane. "I'm not leaving those people."

There were vampires running alongside the APC, jumping up on the side of the vehicle, but it was designed not to let anyone, human or demon, simply burst in.

The APC hit the front steps of the cafeteria and plowed through glass doors and metal frame as well as a handful of vampires in self-consciously ironic MEAT IS MURDER T-shirts as it ripped into the building.

Inside the cafeteria, Alex jerked the steering wheel hard to the right, spinning the vehicle on linoleum tiles and sending cafeteria tables flying. He threw the vehicle in reverse and backed it up.

"What did you find back there, Paul?" Alex shouted.

Paul came forward. "Lead batons and an ax." He held up a couple of police-style batons, red in color, and a fire ax.

"No guns?"

"I'm thinking these guys prefer to fight up close and personal."

Alex hit the brakes as the vehicle came near the cages that hung in the back of the cafeteria.

"Okay, opening the back," he said, flipping a switch on the dashboard. There was a metallic groan as the rear of the vehicle began to roll up like a garage door.

Alex took the ax, handing Minhi his Polibow. "You have about six shots left."

There was a loud growl and Alex looked forward. In front of the vehicle, vampires were climbing up on the hood, heading for the glass.

"How do I keep them from coming through the windshield?" Alex asked aloud, scanning the dashboard. *Think.*

They were vampires. If they traveled in these vans, they couldn't have big glass windshields; the sun might burn them alive. Unless they kept these vehicles inside all day. He was betting vampires planned better than that.

Alex looked around at his controls and found a switch that said SUN SHIELD. He hit it, and suddenly thin, metallic sheets slammed into place across the windshield, severing two of the bald vampire's fingers at the knuckles. The vampire howled in pain.

An image flickered on, projected against the windshield—a video feed of the outside. Of course there were no vampires on it because vampires were invisible to cameras. But at least Alex could see the room.

"Let's get those other captives," he said, running through to the back of the APC.

Alex jumped out the back door, swinging at a vampire that rose up in front of him, bringing the ax against its head. The creature fell back, stunned. Alex hit the first cage and broke the lock.

Some of the captives were struggling to their feet, agitated, grasping. As he got the first cage open, Alex looked at Minhi and Paul. "Look alive, help them in."

The first captive, the woman, was barely strong enough to move, but Paul and Minhi put their arms under her shoulders and dragged her into the vehicle.

There were seven cages in all, and Alex moved fast. Even with Minhi and Paul's help he had to alternate between hacking at the locks and turning to slash at the vampires as they crowded around.

Paul punched one of the vampires in the head with a baton, and it went down but quickly rose again. Alex hit the last lock and began to drag out the final captive, a man in his thirties. Shoving the man into the rear of the APC, Alex saw Minhi strike one vampire across the face with her foot, then raise the Polibow and punch a hole in its chest with a silver bolt. It went up in a flash.

Alex realized they were surrounded—growls coming fast.

A bony white hand caught him by the shoulder. He heard a laugh and turned as a vampire bared her fangs. Alex's heart sank. It was the yellow-haired vampire again. Her shoulder was already healed and she was back for more.

"We're not done," she said. Alex swept at her with the ax but she dodged him—and started to leap for his throat.

An explosion ripped through the air, and suddenly her neck and the side of her face were on fire. The female snarled in pain and fell back as other vampires shrank from the vehicle, their skin burnt.

"What the heck was that?" Alex said.

Paul held up a glass ball of holy water. He must have found it in the backpack. "These things are like antivampire hand grenades."

"Let's go," Alex shouted, climbing up into the APC; he had lost track of the yellow hair. He flipped the door switch and they were already moving as the rear door descended. Minhi brought the ax down on the head of another vampire who was trying to get through the closing door. The creature fell away.

The APC lurched and jumped as Alex steered it through the same hole he had created, and they churned out onto the white grass.

"Is everyone all right?" Alex asked, glancing back. Minhi and Paul were still okay, but the other captives— he had no idea what it would take to help them. Their help would have to come later, from more able hands.

He gritted his teeth as the APC rumbled over a couple of vampires who were trying to jump up on the hood.

Suddenly the APC slid hard to the left. Alex cursed, turning the wheel. There was a powerful sound of something striking the outside and he looked around. They were still barely halfway across the courtyard. "What was that?"

Paul tapped the screen on the windshield. "He's icing the road."

Ice. "This is one of his vans, Paul. They gotta have chains."

"What?"

"Chains, automatic tire chains—if these guys travel with Icemaker, they'll have to have a way to drive these vehicles when he ices the place up."

Alex scanned the dashboard and spotted a switch that said ICE CHAINS, and hit it. Up ahead, toward the iron gate, he could see white layers of ice and snow building up on the ground. Suddenly the APC jumped a bit as the wheels gained traction again.

Heavy staccato sounds came pounding against the hull as Alex aimed for the closed gate. "They're surrounding us," he said flatly. He looked back, scanning the ceiling of the van. "Paul—reach into the pack where you found the glass balls."

"Okay?" Paul was listening.

"Grab a cartridge for my bow and reload it."

Paul was rummaging through the pack and found the cartridges, and took a moment to eject the Polibow's cartridge and pop in a new one. He looked back in the bag and held up a small device the size of a pager. A red light was blinking and making a barely audible beeping sound. "Hey, this thing is beeping, Alex, is this a bomb?"

Alex glanced at it and shook his head. "I have no idea, leave it," Alex said. "Look for the escape hatch in the roof."

Paul looked up and saw the fire-escape-like ladder in the roof. "Okay."

"Bring it down, open the hatch, stick out your head, and shoot some vampires. Be careful; you only have twelve shots."

"You've got to be kidding."

"Paul!"

"Got it." Paul leapt over the seat and grabbed the ladder that was attached by a hinge to the ceiling, yanking it down.

In the back, the other captives stared in disbelief as Paul climbed the ladder. He turned a handle at the roof of the vehicle and flipped open a huge, metal cover, sticking out his head, his arm, and the Polibow.

Paul pumped bolts as the Scholomance gate with its iron S came up fast. They hit the gate hard, sending the iron bars crashing back, and they were finally on the long road up to the top.

Paul was cursing and shooting as Alex steered, flooring it up the grade. Suddenly there was a *slam* and the image on the windshield went dark. Something must have hit the video camera.

Alex flipped the sun shield off and the metal shields fell back.

There were vampires all over the hood.

They were tearing at the windshield, baring their fangs as their fingers managed to punch out chunks of Plexiglas. They were yanking at the metal grid even as their fingers sizzled against it. The metal must be silver, Alex realized. To stop rival vampires. Alex couldn't see the road at all; he scraped against the wall as he drove blind, and he heard Paul shout, "DO NOT CRASH!"

"Can you get these guys off the hood?"

Paul started firing away at the vampires up front, and at least two of them burst into ash and flame, but there were more.

Suddenly, a terrible thought occurred to Alex. They had no way out of the tunnel, or at least he didn't know one. They could hit the edge and crash into the wall, surrounded by vampires. They would be torn apart while they tried to open the magic door. How would they get through the exit? When he had struck it with his fist it had felt like concrete.

Now they hit the last grade, vampires leaping around them, coming up fast on all sides. Alex tried to ignore the vampires on the hood, looking past their shoulders. He could see the end of the tunnel.

"Paul, come inside!" He had no choice. "Brace yourselves!"

Alex floored the accelerator and pounded the APC toward the end of the tunnel and the shimmer of moonlight that he could see showing through the invisible wall.

He looked up ahead as the end of the tunnel came fast. Out there beyond the shimmering wall, Alex saw great arcs of water flying.

Someone was spraying gallons of holy water.

All at once the entrance was sparking and opening up.

Beyond that, Alex saw what appeared to be a thick iron lattice, snapping out across the surface of the lake from the shore, glimmering brightly in the night.

The vehicle slammed through the wall of water with vampires still attached to the hood. Alex closed his eyes, waiting for the impact of the APC falling into the lake. He forced his eyes open in shock as the wheels came down on solid ground—or something solid, anyway.

"What is that?" Paul shouted.

They were driving toward the shore on a *road* that someone had laid from the lip of the tunnel to the land.

"It's a bridge," Alex shouted. He couldn't believe it. But he was *driving* on it! Alex looked out at the iron road that had been rolled out across the water; it was actually floating on hundreds of glistening aluminum pontoons. And then he had another shock: the sight of a Black Hawk helicopter hanging over the shore, waiting to protect their exit.

Alex drove right under the Black Hawk, so close that the APC nearly struck the belly of the chopper as it passed.

Looking up, Alex saw none other than Sangster grin briefly from his place inside the door of the Black Hawk, next to a mounted, Gatling-style, six-barreled M134 Minigun.

Alex heard Sangster's voice booming across the intercom.

"I got this, kid. Proceed out to the road."

As they passed underneath, Sangster spun the Minigun around and tore the heads off the vampires crawling on the vehicle. Alex kept driving, up onto the shore and past the vineyards. In the rearview mirror he saw the helicopter hanging there as Sangster shot hundreds of rounds of wood-and-silver bullets, until the entrance to the Scholomance closed up and disappeared once more.

CHAPTER 22

"How did you know I was driving out?" Alex asked as Sangster ushered him into the bowels of the farmhouse.

The events of the dawn had been a splendid blur. Sangster's colleagues in the Polidorium, though grim faced that Alex had gone in alone on a mission they had never fully supported, took charge of the captives, whom they treated gently. The Polidorium would help with their physical and mental recovery before handing them over to the Swiss police for reunions with their families.

Paul and Minhi had been told, *You don't know who rescued you. Nobody here was anyone you recognize. You never saw the terrorists' faces.* They were now back at their schools—there were headmistresses to be assuaged and parents to be called. Alex himself should have been exhausted, but he was still running on adrenaline. He would have to crash soon, he knew.

"We had a tracker in the go package. By the time you hit the tunnel we knew you were on the way out and moving fast, too fast to be on foot," Sangster said.

Sangster was still limping—but not much, and he had left his cane behind. "You're nearly healed," Alex said, incredulous, as they went through the door and into the carpeted corridors of the Polidorium HQ.

"It was a sprain."

Alex snorted. "Hairline fracture—so how does that work?"

Sangster stopped and Alex did, too. "A long time ago I was offered a choice by the Polidorium. It's a choice you may make one day. But not anytime soon."

"Holy—are you a vampire?"

Sangster rolled his eyes. "The one good vampire in a world of evil?"

"That seems plausible enough."

"Let me tell you something." Sangster stopped, turning to look Alex in the eye. "There are no good vampires, at least none I've ever encountered. Icemaker may have an obsession but he was never all that sympathetic in the first place. It just doesn't work that way. Whatever that person was is perverted by the curse, and no empathy, no feeling, no love in the way *we* know it can remain. Don't ever forget that."

"So you're saying you're not a vampire."

"Surely we have work to do . . ."

"What about a *dhampyr*, like in *Vampire Hunter D*?" Alex asked, remembering Sid's comics.

"*Vampire Hunter* . . . A *half* vampire?" Sangster raised an eyebrow. "I don't know where to start. But I'll say this; the dead don't reproduce—at least not like that," Sangster said.

"But they do travel fast."

"They do travel fast." Sangster nodded.

"You're not going to tell me why you heal faster than normal."

"Not right now, I'm not."

"So what is this?" Alex asked. Sangster was opening the door into the conference room, and Alex saw Carerras and Armstrong waiting.

"This is a debriefing."

"So you got them out," Carerras said flatly. Alex could not tell if he was impressed. "What about Icemaker's plan?"

"He was going to make a sacrifice," Alex said evenly.

"He wanted to raise someone called Claire."

Sangster looked down. "That would be Claire Clairmont, a woman who probably matched Icemaker in life for deviousness. But I had no idea he was so obsessed. If you had asked me what woman did he despise most in his life, I would have said Claire. But then again, if you were to ask me which one would haunt him, the answer would probably be the same."

Armstrong shrugged. "That is how it goes."

Sangster looked back at Alex. "How was he going to do it?"

"There was a ritual," Alex said, finding a seat. A cup of hot chocolate was sitting waiting for him. *Unbelievable.* "In front of a giant keyhole, like in the Polidori story in *Frankenstein*. On the Feast of Our Lady of Sorrows. Icemaker had a scroll, with an animal scepter head on it. He said it had shown him how."

"Aha," Armstrong said. She tapped some keys in the table and brought up an image on the screen. "Is this it?"

The scroll Alex had last seen in the hands of Icemaker was spinning slowly in a 3-D image. "Yes."

She nodded. "Yep. The Scroll of Hermanubis. This was on the *Wayfarer*, the ship Icemaker hit."

Carerras leaned forward. "So Polidori had found the

scroll Icemaker wanted and hidden it away, because he somehow learned that Icemaker would want to use it to cast a spell to raise the dead."

"I think we've been wrong about *Frankenstein*," Sangster said thoughtfully. "I think Polidori had Mary Shelley put the reference to Icemaker's plan, in the guise of the keyhole story, into *Frankenstein* when she reissued it, just in case we lost any other hints. And over the course of time, we *did* lose the other hints."

"Well, Icemaker was furious that we disrupted his ritual," Alex said. "He managed to raise his demon to do this favor, to raise the dead. Nemesis. But I stole the sacrifice."

"Hmmm," Carerras said, folding his arms. "Then I suppose that's it. Rituals require their proper time. If he was supposed to do it on the Feast of Our Lady of Sorrows, he missed his opportunity."

"That's it for now," Sangster agreed.

Alex sipped the hot chocolate. He was famished. "So, is there anything else?"

"There's a lot," Sangster said. "You're the first agent to make it in and out of that place alive in nearly fifty years."

Alex's heart sank. He was tired. He didn't want to spend another six hours describing the whole ordeal.

And then he realized what Sangster had just called him. An *agent*.

"Not now, though," Sangster said. "Go home. It's done. We'll get the details later."

"Hermanubis, huh?"

Early the next evening, Sid paced the three boys' room as he stared at a mound of books.

Alex had crashed and slept for about seven hours. Paul had been returned to the school in a limo the school sent to the hospital, where he was greeted with cheers and applause by his fellow students—even Merrill & Merrill—all relieved to have him back from his "kidnapping by terrorists." True to his word, Paul stuck to the story. Until he, Sid, and Alex headed back to the room, where they told Sid everything, from the vampire in the woods to the tunnel out of the Scholomance.

"Yeah, it was called the Scroll of Hermanubis," Alex said.

"That makes sense," Sid said. "Hermanubis was an Egyptian god who could move between the world of the living and the dead."

Rather than feeling as though all had gone smashingly—as Alex was inclined to think it had—Sid seemed more ill at ease than ever.

"What is it?" Alex insisted.

Sid heaved a sigh and stared at the desk where he'd tossed every book he could find on Icemaker, his poems, the Haunted Summer, all of it. "I don't know," he said. "Everything in the story in Mary Shelley's *Frankenstein*, in the introduction—it *means* something. The skull-headed lady. The keyhole. All of it was a clue. The skull-headed lady is Claire, whom Icemaker wanted to raise. The demon he needed to help him came through the keyhole."

"Right," said Alex.

"Which makes sense. But we've got a problem."

Paul sat up from where he'd been lying on his bed. "What?"

"If everything in the clue means something, then *everything* in it means something."

"Okay . . ."

Sid opened his copy of *Frankenstein*, thumbing back to the 1831 introduction. "So what about the Tomb of the Capulets?"

"I don't follow." Alex rubbed his eyes with his palms, suddenly feeling very much like he wished he followed even less.

Sid was holding up the book, reading. "The Tomb of the Capulets. Mary Shelley says that after Polidori started writing about the skull lady, *he*—that's Polidori—'*did not know what to do with her and was obliged to despatch her to the tomb of the Capulets, the only place for which she was fitted.*'"

"So?"

Sid picked up another book, this one on the Villa Diodati party of 1816. "You saw Icemaker down in the Scholomance at a keyhole window; that's where Nemesis came. But . . . that was a castle, not a tomb. So there was no Tomb of the Capulets. And it . . . here"— he went to another book and flipped the pages for a moment—"there was a collection of art in 1816, in the house Icemaker rented. The Villa Diodati. There was a painting of the death of Romeo and Juliet."

"*The Tomb of the Capulets,*" repeated Paul.

"Icemaker," Sid said, "when he was Byron, wrote a poem about going to Nemesis. And the whole point of it was that he was a greater kind of being, that he alone was sufficient. I have no doubt that he needed the ritual to perform, and that the scroll held that ritual. But I don't think he needed the captives—the sacrifice—at all."

"What do you mean he didn't need us?" Paul demanded.

"It's—" Sid stood up, pacing. He looked at Alex. "Look, I hate to break this to you, but vampires aren't stupid.

This was a *trick*. He knew you were watching him. When did the Polidorium start tracking Icemaker?"

"The moment he started moving up Italy. He travels with an army, so the Polidorium can't miss him."

"Right—if you're Icemaker, you *know* you're being watched. He had to come to Lake Geneva because the Scholomance was the place to do his ritual, but he knew the heat would be on the moment the caravan started moving. The good guys would want to stop him, to disrupt whatever he was planning. So he made you all part of the plan: stole some captives so you could rescue them and think you disrupted his ritual. You'd go away satisfied. But you didn't disrupt him at all. You gave him time to finish."

"What do you mean, 'to finish'?" Alex asked.

"A vampire rises fully formed out of the grave," Sid said. "But raising a dead human, from dust to bones, to a new being—that takes time, like a day, and room. He triggered it all on midnight of the feast day. It's *not* done. Claire *will rise* at *The Tomb of the Capulets*—the painting—you see?"

"See what?" demanded Alex.

"Claire will rise at the Villa Diodati," Sid said. "She's probably rising *now*."

CHAPTER 23

A hard, pelting rain began to fall as Alex hurtled down the road, the sound of the gunmetal gray Ninja a distant roar inside his muffling helmet. He spoke into the mouthpiece again as he headed north back toward the Villa Diodati. "Sangster, this is Alex. Sangster!"

He cursed as it went to voice mail. Of course, because the job was over. Chains of lightning began to dance across the sky.

Alex left the Ninja against a tree in the vineyard, stopping to grab what he could out of the saddle case. He found the Polibow and what appeared to be a wrist guard lined with silver knives. He wound his way to a basement window and gingerly forced it open.

There was a moment, as Alex dropped down and peered through the window, rain beating on his shoulders, that he doubted his purpose. But it was just a moment. *See this through.* He felt this to be his calling as surely as he felt he had ended up here for a reason. Sangster had said his father had no idea the Polidorium was even at Lake Geneva. So he was here by destiny. His very name had led him here.

Alex's feet struck the floor and he allowed his eyes to adjust to the faint light that came in through the window. For a moment his heart raced as he saw a tall, rakish figure in the corner. He felt himself crouch and then realized it looked rakish because it was, in fact, a rake.

Save your mad skills for the actual monsters, Alex.

This basement room was around the back of the house, and after a moment he could see that it was used primarily for gardening supplies—in the corner he could see a wheelbarrow, some large plastic bags of mulch, various shovels and rakes and other implements of destruction.

Alex stepped out of that room into a basement hallway, where almost no light intruded.

At the other end of the hall Alex saw a dim red light glowing, casting strange shadows across the darkened floor.

In the distance he heard a deep, smooth voice calling:

"But first, on earth as vampire sent,
Thy corse shall from its tomb be rent . . ."

Alex moved toward the end of the hall and stopped, looking slowly around the corner. This hallway was wide, and at the end was a painting.

It covered the entire wall at the end of the corridor: Romeo and Juliet lay in each other's arms before the door of the tomb of the Capulets, with lilies strewn about at their feet. And the door to the tomb was an actual door. Below the door, burning bright, was the eerie red light that filled the hallway.

The mellifluous voice continued:

"Then ghastly haunt thy native place,
And suck the blood of all thy race."

Staring at the door, Alex felt all of his certainty drain away. The whispering static in his brain and the smell of decay hit him and he lost it, retreating and smacking his back against the wall. He started to gasp and couldn't breathe.

The world won't slow down, but your mind can. Ask the questions.

What's going on?

There's something going on through that door.

Something awful and dark.

What do you have?

I have myself, my bow, and my wits.

Can you turn back?

Yes.

Do you want to turn back?

Absolutely not.

Forward. Alex moved rapidly down the hall until he reached the faux tomb door, and found that it had no handle, but pushed, like a kitchen door.

He put his shoulder to the door and swung it open, bracing himself against the growing smell. Inside, at the far wall, he saw two figures immersed in a deed of strange horror.

In a circle of glittering blood that glowed with its own vampiric force, one figure kneeled on the ground, bent and drinking from what Alex took at first to be a bird feeder, it was such a large, wide goblet. The figure wore a shroud and veil. Her face inside the veil, eyeless and skinless—*Skull-headed,* Alex thought—was dipped in the blood and drinking.

The second figure was tall, with hooflike legs of ice, clad in red, his long hair now pulled back, his hand on the veiled woman's shoulder. *Icemaker.* The pose of the vampire and the skull-headed lady suggested nothing so much to Alex as a child compelling a kitten to partake of a saucer of milk.

"My ichor, my body," whispered the clan lord. "Take it in, beloved, O Claire, take it in and join me."

Shaking, Alex raised the Polibow and cocked it, getting Icemaker's attention.

Claire, the newly raised, looked up. Her skull face, obscured by the gauzy veil, dripped with the glittering blood of Icemaker. Alex shot one bolt and caught the skeleton in the sternum, sending it tumbling back.

Icemaker looked in horror at the fallen skeleton and then turned to Alex, baring his fangs. Alex fired again and Icemaker held out his hand. A bolt of air as cold and hard as a hammer smacked Alex's arm, tossing the weapon aside.

The lord shot forward in a single, fluid motion, grabbing Alex up like a puppy. Alex felt his skin pulled tight as the vampire's claws dug into the back of his neck, dragging him across the floor.

"You think this is your destiny, is that it?" the nobleman said as Alex fought against his iron grip. The skin of Alex's neck was screaming in pain. "That you were put on this earth to vex me?"

His voice had that strange sound of raggedness, ice and water.

Alex sucked in air, then managed to say, "You have vexed yourself. You have damned yourself."

"If I have damned myself then God does not need warriors like *you*," the vampire replied. He stopped, holding Alex a few inches off the ground. "If Heaven is His to rule then the suffering wrought by my kind should be of no concern to Him."

"And yet," Alex said, managing to shrug, "here we are." The vampire was going to kill him. *Think. What do you have?*

Icemaker brought Alex close and spoke to him. Not a jot of breath came from him as he rasped, "You don't understand. Polidori did not understand. No Van Helsing could understand. This earth, cold and desolate though it is, is *ours* to rule. Come, and find your reward in the *next* world."

Icemaker dragged Alex over to the gauzy skeleton he had just raised, who lay there on the floor, staring eyeless.

Icemaker held Alex aloft, and now brought up a razor-sharp thumb. "My companion needs more blood," he whispered.

What do you have?

I don't have a damn thing.

Alex felt the thumb make contact with his neck and

dig in. He started to scream when suddenly Icemaker himself hissed in pain as a grappling hook dug into his hand and he yanked it back.

Alex fell to the ground next to the skeleton, slamming into the wide feeder of the Byronic blood and spilling it. Icemaker roared wordlessly, looking up from where the bolt had come.

Paul was peering through a basement window. He had shot a grappling gun and now was pulling with all his might at the cord. Sid, behind him, waved Alex toward them.

"Alex! Let's go!"

Alex was drenched, sickened by the powerful, sweet scent of the clan lord's own glistening, cold ichor wafting up as it soaked through his pants and shirt. He ran out through the painting's door back into the dark hallway, finding stairs up into the main foyer of the villa.

Alex could hear a helicopter out on the lawn. They had gotten his message.

When he got upstairs, Alex dashed toward Sangster, who was running in the front entrance. Behind Sangster, Alex saw Agent Armstrong in the doorway quickly working with some kind of metal tank, using a drill to bolt it to the doorjamb.

"Icemaker's down there!" Alex shouted to Sangster,

who was nodding that he knew. "He didn't need the blood of the captives after all; he just needed his own blood. It was enough of a sacrifice for Nemesis and enough to do the raising. But he didn't finish. She's just a *skull-headed lady*!"

Sangster pointed him out the door. Alex headed past Armstrong in the doorway with the drill, and now he saw that it wasn't just a single tank but several, situated all around the entrance. Armstrong signaled him to keep moving, and he did, out the front, to where a Polidorium Black Hawk rested on the lawn.

Alex ran around to the low basement-access window to find Paul and Sid standing back, while Polidorium agents clustered around the opening to keep Icemaker from coming out.

"You followed me?" Alex said, still shocked.

"Of course," Paul said.

"Where did you get a grappling gun?" Alex exclaimed.

"Out of your amazing Technicolor dream backpack," Sid answered, handing it to Alex. "You left it on that motorcycle. And since when do you have a motorcycle?"

Looking into the window of the basement, Alex could see Icemaker still tugging against the cord when

Sangster came in through the door from the hallway. As Sangster entered, firing, Icemaker sent an angry blast of ice that covered over the basement window.

"Hey!" Alex heard Sangster shout. They heard two more shots.

A few moments later, Alex heard Sangster running for the door. "Here he comes!" the agent shouted as he moved across the marble floors toward the entrance.

Sangster hit the entryway and leapt out, past Armstrong, who now rolled away from the doorway with a large metal switch in her hand. Inside, the vampire was coming up the stairs, roaring. Alex left Paul and Sid and moved toward the helicopter, gripping his Polibow.

"He is hauling ass," Sangster said.

Alex saw Armstrong look back through the doorway one last time. Just as Icemaker's head was topping the stairs that ran down to the lower level, the vampire saw her, and as his arms came up he fired a blast of ice, hitting Armstrong hard in the shoulder and sending her flying off the porch.

Armstrong lay on the ground, stunned, her shoulder frozen. Sangster swore loudly as Icemaker started making his way across the enormous foyer. The vampire looked down at his chest as Sangster's hawthorn bullets smacked into his armored doublet and he again held up his hand, raging. Air swirled and froze around his hand. He sent another blast.

Sangster caught the column of ice on the arm, and it forced him back a dozen yards into the chopper, freezing his hand and forearm there. His Beretta clattered uselessly to the grass.

Alex had no time to worry about Sangster—his eyes drew toward the switch Armstrong had dropped. They were going to lose Icemaker. Alex reached into the door of the Black Hawk and scanned. Against the wall was a netting laced with straps of glass balls. He grabbed a glass ball and bounded for the porch, taking two steps at a time. For a moment he took shelter behind a column on the porch and judged the distance. Then he jumped out, throwing. The ball sailed in a clean arc toward Icemaker.

It landed smack against Icemaker's chest, tinkling into shards and sending deadly rivulets of holy water against the vampire's neck and face.

Icemaker staggered back. "You!" he cried.

Alex brought the Polibow up and fired, striking Icemaker twice in the shoulder. The shafts stuck there, steam rising off Icemaker as angrily he held up his hand. The air started to cool and swirl. He was going to fire. Alex dived across the porch for the switch as a cold blast of ice shot past, shattering the tips of his hair. He landed next to the door and smacked the switch just as Icemaker leapt across the entryway of the house. As the vampire crossed the threshold, the tanks Alex triggered struck the vampire with a burst of nitrogen. Huge blasts showered down at once, enveloping him.

The vampire moved across the porch, slowing as he looked around in shock.

Icemaker let out a painful howl that shook the porch. The vampire made eye contact with Alex for a moment. Alex studied him—the look he saw was not fear, not pain, but raw frustration and anger. *That's right*, thought Alex. *A Van Helsing has beaten you.*

Icemaker seemed to make up his mind, growing eerily defiant and calm as he stopped fighting the nitrogen. Suddenly he looked Alex again in the eye, calmly. The air froze around him. Layer upon layer built up at once, until he was not to be seen. He would hibernate rather than suffer direct nitrogen encasement, which might freeze the vampire's cells more deeply than even he could deal with. Within moments, Lord Byron, the Icemaker, had become a block, Lord Byron, the Ice.

CHAPTER 24

Speaking of ice . . . Alex sat in Secheron's ice-cream parlor for the second time in his life, this time joined not just by Minhi, Paul, and Sid but also by Sangster.

"So where is he being kept?" Alex asked.

"We have refrigerated places," Sangster said. "You don't want to know where." Sangster had decided he would speak as plainly as possible about his second job with the present company, mainly because they had already witnessed most of the pertinent stuff. He was protected by the insanity of what they might try to reveal—for who would believe any of it?

"Is this like in *The Blob*," Alex asked, "where you attach a parachute to him and drop him in the Arctic?"

"*The Blob*?" Minhi said, as she sat holding hands with

Paul. Alex felt an utterly tiny pang of jealousy. "That's the best you can do, a fifty-year-old movie reference?"

"The Arctic is a lot warmer than it was when that movie was made, so any frozen monster dropped off there runs the risk of not staying frozen long." Sangster sighed. "But that reminds me that we need to be on the lookout for the Blob. There's always one more thing." He laughed.

Alex nodded. One more thing. The Polidorium had discovered that the lake entrance to the Scholomance near the Villa Diodati was gone. The demonic school was unreachable for now.

Carerras had agreed not to call Alex's father, after Alex pleaded with him. For now, that was a favor the Polidorium was willing to extend in thanks for his help stopping a clan lord. Alex himself would have to decide how to proceed with Dad. Since Dad had gone to so much trouble to cover up Alex's first (unknowing) attack on a supernatural creature, he would surely whisk Alex out of here as well. And Alex wanted anything but that. Not with the Polidorium still in place. Not with these friends.

"What about the skeleton?" Alex asked. It was something that had been bothering him since that night, and of course he had not been able to go back down into the Villa Diodati, which had been cordoned off. The Polidorium's cover story was that a tree had damaged the porch in the storm. "What about Claire?"

Sangster shrugged. "We're watching," he said. "But she hasn't turned up."

This didn't happen: Alex Van Helsing didn't stop all his vampire hunting training and turn instead to a quiet life of contemplation and study. That *might* have happened— in an infinite universe that had to happen sometimes— but it didn't happen this time.

Because far below the waters of the lake, the Scholomance had other plans.

"We will each write a ghost story," said Lord Byron; and his proposition was acceded to. . . . Poor Polidori had some terrible idea about a skull-headed lady, who was so punished for peeping through a key-hole—what to see I forget—something very shocking and wrong of course; but when she was reduced to a worse condition than the renowned Tom of Coventry, he did not know what to do with her, and was obliged to despatch her to the tomb of the Capulets, the only place for which she was fitted. . . .

I busied myself to think of a story.

—Mary Shelley, *Frankenstein*, Introduction, 1831 ed.